TREASURE in the FLAME

To DonnaLee
Happy reading,
Brenda Corey Dunne,

BRENDA COREY DUNNE

fortunate frog fiction

First Print Edition: August 2012

ISBN-13: 978-0-9881562-1-0

Editor: Jesse Steele
Proofreader: Wendy Dunlop Marr
Cover Photo: David Corey
Cover Design: Streetlight Graphics, http://www.streetlightgraphics.com/

DEDICATION

*In memory of
Dr. Margaret Jean Corey,
who taught me to believe.
(1939-2002)*

PROLOGUE

THE OPPORTUNITY PRESENTED ITSELF IN the form of a map. Just a piece of parchment on the ale-soaked wooden floor of a Sainte Anne's pub, more than likely dropped by a drunkard on his way home to his hungry wife. Finder's keepers, Jonas told himself as he bent down and scooped it up.

It was a treasure map.

Not just any treasure map, but *the* Treasure Map: the source of endless local whispers of mystery, gold and curses, of treasure and death on the Koac Stream. He was sure of it.

To Jonas the map was hope. Hope for his daughter in the form of a ticket back to England and a future away from crusty mill workers. Almost a woman, she deserved a good education and a fine home, and the treasure would help to pay for them. So he gathered four trusted friends and, in the blackness of the new moon, set out on a treasure hunt. The map wasn't easy to follow. Somehow, whether through fate, divine intervention or just sheer luck, they found the spot.

Thunk-shht. Thunk-shht.

The shovel's call shouted through the silence. Metal against dirt, man against nature deep in a hidden cave.

They dug in enforced silence...just in case.

After Jonas's second turn at the shovel he began to doubt. It was getting late. Soon the sun would rise. Maybe this wasn't the place. He had to get home for Aminda. He shouldn't have left her alone.

When no treasure emerged after another hour of shovelling, he motioned to the men that he was leaving. Disgust at himself tamed his obsession. He did not need gold. He needed to get back to his daughter. He could always come back.

With angry gesticulations they demanded he stay, their fervour and fear warring in silence. They were men possessed; the undeniable call of gold was flowing in their veins. He shook his head and pulled out his pocketwatch, pointing at the time. He found a candle and lit it. Then he walked away.

The *thunk-shht* followed him.

The sound was eerie, like the chained steps of the undead. He held the candle high, but its flickering light did little to dispel the darkness. Whispers slipped from the cave walls. One fork in the cave, then two...then eight, he followed in reverse their shadowy footsteps. Still the echo of shovelling ricocheted around him.

Thunk-shht. Thunk...shht.

Clink.

"There it is...is...is...is...!"

The voice shot past him like an arrow.

He spun towards the sound. Someone had spoken. Someone had broken the silence. A puff of air caressed his face, snuffing out his candle.

Fear crawled down his neck.

A slow growl, like an angry demon, rolled toward him. It grew, the sound of a thousand hurricanes, the agony of a thousand deaths. The tortured screams of men stung his ears. The ground shook as the sound bellowed through the cave, rushing toward him.

Jonas Ingerham turned and ran for his life.

CHAPTER 1

ALMOST ALONE

AMINDA SAT IN THE SUNLIGHT, resting her head on the weather-beaten wooden rail. Her feet dangled over the dam, skirts billowing in the gentle breeze. There was no one around to waggle their fingers at her so she let them go—heedless of the glimpse of ankle she was giving the pool below. The water wheel turned aimlessly, its *wush-wush-wush* a whisper of its regular racket. Fifty-eight fine straight logs lay atop the headpond, waiting their turn at the blade. She knew there were fifty-eight because she had counted them, as she had every day since her father had opened the mill. Today they lay silent in the Sunday sun.

Sunday afternoon. All of the good families were gathering around their tables, saying grace over their simple meals before heading off for their second round of hell and brimstone at the meeting house. Aminda had had enough damnation for one day. This morning at services she had feigned a headache—she smiled at the thought. Let the gossiping ladies chew on that awhile. She had no desire to go back into the steamy hall. Besides, her meal would be depressing enough without the added Sunday guilt.

She shouldn't have left her father alone in the cabin, but Aunt Mary had gone home to her family and the day had been so lovely that Aminda hadn't wanted to lose it. A few minutes of peace here on the dam and then she'd head up to the cabin to check on him. She just needed a little break from the darkness and still air.

The sun warmed her face. The stream babbled below. And then her peace was shattered by the sound of footsteps.

For Mercy's sake, could she not have just a few minutes to herself?

She crossed her dangling legs demurely, hoping to salvage some decency. The footsteps grew louder and then slowed as the boards beneath her vibrated with their force.

"Miss Ingerham." The voice was deep, musical. She recognized it and blushed. Of all the voices in this Godforsaken place, it was one of the few she actually *wanted* to hear, and the one the villagers would least like her to. Not that she cared for their opinions. And anyway, there was no escaping it; common courtesy dictated a reply.

"Mr. O'Brien." She looked up. The sunlight shadowed his face. Tall, muscular and freckled. The Irishman's son looked down on her with compassion. The jumpy twitching in her stomach deepened Aminda's red cheeks.

"I'm sorry, am I disturbin' you?" he asked, Irish accent just touching the words as he said them. "I suspect you could use with a bit o' peace, after all of the old biddies tut-tutting about you. Would you like me to leave?"

She would not. "No, it's all right. I don't mind. I was just getting a breath of fresh air."

"Your father? Any change?"

"No. The same."

He stood silently for a few minutes, looking down towards the stream.

4

"I'm sorry," he said then, his voice filled with true compassion.

Without asking, he sat down beside her, only the rail separating them. She snuck a glance. His eyelashes glinted in the sunlight and the dirt he normally sported had been washed away—Saturday night bath, no doubt. Even his britches were clean.

Patrick was the oldest of six, maybe seven? And there were rumours of another on the way. Aminda knew that they scraped by with a drunkard of a father and little else. Patrick, at sixteen, was the reason they survived.

The O'Briens didn't attend meetings in the village. And to all of the villagers who did, Patrick and his family were flat-out heathens—a dangerous accusation in this tiny little place. Aminda knew better. Patrick was kinder and more Godlike than most of them could ever hope to be.

He turned and smiled at her.

"I am sorry...about your da. He is a good man, Mr. Ingerham."

The kindness in his voice was worth more than a million tut-tutting old biddies. It tore at her heart. She looked away. The stream beneath them meandered lazily towards the river. A waft of wood smoke crept over the trees in the afternoon sun.

"He sleeps...not really ill, not really well," she said hesitantly. She was glad to speak to someone, and in truth no one else had asked. Well, asked like Patrick was asking—as if they really cared what the answer was. "Just sleep, nothing else. The doctor from the Fort doesn't help. He gives me powders and draughts, but none of them work..."

Yes, the fool had given her powders—plenty of powders—all the time blathering pompously on about ague and consumption and weak hearts. But her father was a strong man, and he had fallen sick without warning. No fever, no

5

chills. One day he was fine, and the next day... he wasn't. Sometimes he muttered strange words of fear in his unnatural slumber. He spoke of curses and treasure before falling silent once more.

She didn't want him to die. She wasn't ready for the world on her own.

"Some say as it's a curse," Patrick said, his voice barely a whisper.

She looked at him sharply. She'd heard the rumours; Aunt Mary, the men at the mill, the ladies at church. Mostly quick whispers behind her back. Patrick held her gaze, not challenging, but questioning.

"Some say as it's a curse that has to do with gold."

She had heard that too.

"Yes, some say that," she replied warily. She looked away again, avoiding his gaze. The slow *wush-wush* of the idling waterwheel soothed her frayed nerves. Patrick's implied question did not.

She had watched her father leave from the shadows of the loft that night days ago. Wondering why her father was going out so late, she had followed and hidden in the branches beside the dam. At least four other men walked down to the stream with her father, slipping into the small ketch anchored there. Not recognizing any of them in the dim light, she had returned to her bed, confused.

"It must be hard for you, keeping the mill with everything else," Patrick said, his voice unpleasantly interrupting unpleasant memories.

Anger flashed hot in her chest.

"Yes, Mr. O'Brien," she said through clenched teeth. "It is hard. I have a home, land, and a father to look after. I am alone... for now. But my father will recover, and I will not bow to men's talk."

She had thought Patrick O'Brien different... but, no. He was just like the others who wanted her mill. She was fifteen years old and just as capable of running it as any man. Her father had at least given her that.

Enough.

She stood, stomping her feet on the wooden boards to shake her skirts down. "I can do quite well without your pity," she said, the warmth of the moment drifting away like the wood smoke as she glared at him.

He held up his hand. "No. Aminda, wait! I didna mean to imply. I only wanted to offer my help! My own da would have the mill from you if he could, as would many others. But not me."

She waited, hands on her hips and eyebrows raised.

He stood, slowly and methodically. The same way he did everything, she thought. His hand, large and calloused, gripped the railing before he spoke.

"I know what it's like to stand alone against many."

"Yes..." she huffed.

"I just wanted to say...sometimes, when the whole world seems against you, it helps to have a body to talk to."

Aminda stared at him, not sure what lay behind his words.

"And you're offering to be that body?"

"Aye, I am." His eyes shone the blue of Atlantic icebergs.

He was right, though. She desperately needed a friend in all of this madness. But, Patrick? She liked him, sure, but how did she know she could trust him? She knew so little about him, and what she did was the result of village gossip.

"I'll think about it," she said.

He tipped his cap and made to walk by.

"I'm working in the west pasture of late," was all he said before striding away across the dam, leaving Aminda to her thoughts in the afternoon sun.

His offer simmered beneath her skin as she walked
home along the steep shaded road toward to their cabin, the
evening chill sinking through her sweater. Though it was the
last week of May, frost was still a possibility here on the River
St. John. She wrapped her arms around herself and looked
up, just once, before following the path to the cabin.

High above the cabin, the half-finished shell of the 'Big
House' overlooked the mill and the stream as it emptied into
the river. Her father had begun building it in the spring,
just after the snow melted. It looked down at now her like
a forgotten promise. Its true second story and proper cellar
for cold storage were luxuries she would have to wait for.
She longed to have proper walls, a proper hearth and glazed
windows, but it would not happen this year. Strong and
knowledgeable as she was, she couldn't build a house like
that on her own. She sighed and turned away. The stuffy,
dimly-lit, bare-log cabin they lived in now would have to do.

Her father had not changed. He lay as if dead, a shadow of
his former self. The quilts were unruffled and his slow, even
breaths came and went like the tide. The hearth glowed with
broken coals, warming the cabin against the chill spring air.
Aminda walked to her father's side and sat on the bed beside
him, gently placing her hand on his forehead. It was cool
and dry.

"Father, I'm back," she whispered. She was afraid to wake
him but hopeful she would.

There was no response. His chest rose and fell, rose
and fell.

"I met up with Patrick O'Brien," she said. Now why had
she told him that? She supposed it was guilt. Proper young

women did not meet up with single young men without a chaperone, especially on Sunday afternoons. Mind you, there weren't many people whom she could ask to perform that duty now, were there? Her mother was long dead and she had no older siblings—no siblings at all, for that matter. Aunt Mary visited only because of an overdeveloped sense of duty. Anyway, the thought of Aunt Mary chaperoning while she met with a suitor made her skin crawl.

Aminda got up and walked to the hearth, stirring the coals quickly and adding a few small sticks. When the wood caught, she swung the waiting pot of leftover stew over the fire, stirring it without looking and then moving away. Perhaps if her mother were here, she wouldn't be in this predicament. Her father might not have even left the cabin that night a week ago. But there was no use wishing for things she couldn't have. Mother was dead. Three years dead. Josephine Ingerham had died giving birth to Aminda's unnamed brother, the very day they began their journey from Connecticut.

And so her mother had not been here to prevent her father from leaving in the dark of night. Aminda ladled some stew into a wooden bowl, remembering the wee hours of that morning a week ago. When her father returned from wherever he had gone, he was not well. He murmured incomprehensibly of men, shovels and moonlight. Just before he fell silent, he grabbed her arm. "You mustn't speak!" he demanded. "Go by moonlight! Beware the Whitebeard!" His eyes were wide, the corners of his mouth flecked with spittle. And then he collapsed.

She searched his body for marks, but there was no visible reason for his unnatural sleep. No bruises, cuts or fever, only a graze on his knuckles and that wasn't uncommon for a lumberman. Her only clue was the small piece of parchment she had found clutched in his hand.

A treasure map.

CHAPTER 2

AVOIDANCE

As the evening shadows grew long, Aminda finished her meal and stoked the fire again. She took the slop to the pigs, gave hay to the cows and horses and locked the brooding hens away for the night. Turtle the cat rubbed at her legs as she carried eggs in her apron.

"Hello Turt," Aminda said. She reached down to scratch his ears. "Catch any mice today?" The cat purred in response.

Her father tolerated the cat, but Aminda loved him dearly. His name was a tribute to the markings on his back. She allowed him to follow her into the cabin and set a small bowl of milk down by his favourite spot. Her father would never know the cat had been inside and the creature was a small comfort in her bizarre, chaotic life.

She washed her dish, then mashed a small amount of stew in it.

"Father, you must try to eat," she said.

She patted his cheeks, gently then more firmly. "Father, wake up..."

Nothing.

"Mr. Ingerham!"

He slept on.

"Jonas!" Aminda tried his given name, mimicking the memory of her mother's loving tone. Though nothing worked, she spooned a small amount of stew mush into her father's mouth. He remained still. She pressed his lips closed and rubbed his throat.

He swallowed.

Aminda nearly dropped the spoon in surprise.

"Father? Can you hear me?"

Nothing.

She tried the same technique. He swallowed again. He made no other movements, but Aminda managed to slowly feed him the entire bowl.

Perhaps all was not lost.

⟋⟋⟋⟍⟍⟍

For as long as Aminda could remember, she had faced away from the fire. She hated tending it. Her mother had nicknamed her 'Sweater Girl' because she would rather wear three sweaters than sit near the hearth. On the day her family fled Connecticut Aminda finally realized why. Her mother, frantic with packing, had put her in charge of the meal. It was while she was stirring that it happened.

The flames called to her, pulled her in. So she looked.

Tired and frightened by the angry men outside, she had forgotten her aversion. Her eyes slipped from the hanging pot to the fire below. Orange fingers sucked at her consciousness, and in the flickering light her mother's face appeared—contorted in pain, then slack in death.

Aminda dropped the spoon into the coals.

"Clumsy girl!" her mother scolded. "Pick it out and wash it!" Aminda stood there, open-jawed in shock. Had anyone else seen the face in the fire?

"Aminda Jane! Do you hear me? Pick out the spoon and wash it!"

"But..." Aminda's eyes flashed from her mother's face to the coals and back again.

"Now, child!"

Aminda did as she was told.

Her mother died that very night.

∾⦚⦚∽

The crowing rooster cut through Aminda's sleep—jagged and insistent. She jumped from her small bed in the loft, much to Turtle's dismay. He yowled at her as he stretched.

"Sorry, Turt." She dressed quickly in a rumpled calico dress and rushed down the steep stairwell from the loft. Eyes habitually turned away, she stirred the coals and added some broken cedar planks, cast-offs of the mill. Her father lay unmoving.

When the fire felt right, she swung the iron pot over it to heat water for washing and breakfast. She pushed the tallow pot closer to the coals and wiped her hands on her apron. Satisfied that all was well, she headed out to do the morning chores.

Rain fell, making the barnyard a mucky mess. There were two cows to milk, eggs to gather, and hay to feed. She turned the horses out into the paddock and rushed back inside. The fire was low, but the water was hot. She added more wood, ladling a little water into a basin to wash with before adding oats to the pot.

Half an hour later her father swallowed his gruel but did not wake.

Aunt Mary arrived in a foul mood, splattering muck onto

Aminda's just-swept floor. She mumbled as she hung her shawl on the hook, shooting dirty looks Aminda's way.

"Any change?" she demanded as if it were Aminda's fault that her father didn't wake up. Aminda wondered why her Aunt bothered to come at all. Perhaps her boar of a husband wanted an update? Aminda was sure he wanted the mill.

"No. The same," she said through gritted teeth. In essence he was that, the same. Even though he had swallowed some gruel and some stew, he stayed frozen in that half-alive place.

"Well then, get on with you. I expect the men will be waiting." Aunt Mary flounced herself down in the rocking chair by the fire and pulled out her mending, dismissing Aminda with a flick of her hand.

Aminda rolled her eyes, tied on her bonnet and slipped through the door without a backward glance. Aunt Mary's derogatory tone pricked at her temper. The woman was an opinionated menace. There was no question as to how she felt about Aminda's refusal to give up the keys to the mill. No one had asked outright yet, but it had been implied more than once. Aminda kept them on a string beneath her bodice as a sort of insurance. As long as the men needed her to get in, they needed her to do their work. If they did not work, they would not get paid. The key to the money box was also on her breast. As scandalous as the village ladies thought it was, she also held the keys to the cupboard which held the cask of rum—rum the men were given as partial payment for their day's work. As she walked down the hill she held the bucket of hot tallow to use as grease for the mechanisms of the saw mill.

She didn't know how long it would last, but while her father still lived she would let no one else hold the keys, and she would continue to bring the tallow pot each morning.

Curling pipe smoke rose from the eaves of the mill. The

men stood beneath the covered loading dock, smoking pipes and grumbling. Her approach silenced them.

"Good morning, gentlemen," she said through the smoky haze. Gentlemen, they were not. But she would call them so just the same.

They nodded, their faces silently mocking.

"Mr. Jones. If you would step aside, please," she said as she gestured toward the door.

The look he gave her was not friendly at all. Mr. Jones was blatantly against women in the mill. She would rather step barefooted on a rusty nail than speak politely to him but she held her tight smile. He nodded and stepped to the side.

Aminda willed her hands not to shake as she moved past them. She pulled the keys from her bodice as discreetly as she could. The hot bucket of tallow steamed as it swung from her other hand. One of the men chuckled behind her back.

"Would you like some help with that, Miss?" Mr. Jones asked with his eyes on her chest.

He was vile. He stank of unwashed male and last night's onions. "I thank you, but no," she replied, injecting as much venom as she could into her voice.

"No need to get touchy, Miss. Just offerin' to help's all," he said as the others jeered behind her.

"You can save your energy for your work, Mr. Jones," she said, and unlocked the door.

The smell of fresh-cut pine cleaned her lungs as she walked through the door. There were many happy memories in this place. Her father showing her how to place the beams and how to hammer a nail. Nights of sweeping sawdust as he greased the machinery. Lunches of cold meat and warm biscuits. A sip of strong rum from his cup. She had helped him build this mill. She knew each and every part of the machinery and could fix it in a pinch. The men behind her hated her for it. A lumber mill was not the place for a skirt and braids.

As the men hung their lunch pails and their damp wool coats, Aminda walked up the stairs to the main level and checked the gears. The saw slide needed a touch of tallow, so she dabbed it with a brush. The sluice gate lever awaited her call.

She pulled her father's pocketwatch from her apron.

"I mark two minutes to eight," she said, making her voice as deep and as forceful as she could. "Lunch and a dram at noon. I'll return then." She nodded to the foreman, Mr. Stairs. He walked outside and as he pulled the lever to raise the sluice gate the machinery roared to life. Aminda nodded again. The sound never failed to stir her. It was useless to try and talk above the din, so without another glance she walked past the men, unlocked the upper door and walked out onto the dam. Mr. Stairs tipped his hat at her on the way by.

Aminda liked Mr. Stairs most of all. He was the least likely to cause a fuss. Perhaps it was because he had four daughters of his own or because he had known Aminda the longest. He knew that she understood the workings of the mill. And he knew that she would not give up until her father was cold in a grave.

The mist was cool on her face and calming to her nerves. She stood there for a few seconds, breathing in the musty scents of the pool and the sharp tang of pine while counting logs. Fifty-seven now—the first log was down the chute. The steely whine of the saw confirmed it.

Was it just yesterday she had sat here with Patrick O'Brien? The days were blurring together. She could use a friend right now—someone who wouldn't judge her by village standards. But an O'Brien? Spurned by the local community for their religious beliefs, his family had been given the farthest grant from the village. They had arrived flea-bitten, crawling with lice and half-starved, and then been forced to build their own road to access their land. Patrick fit in here even less than she did. She wouldn't have minded him as a friend. Or more. Her cheeks warmed as she thought of his tanned and freckled face.

Friendship or not, she would not be walking to his west pasture in the rain. The village had enough to gossip about. She turned and strode back toward the cabin, wet skirts swishing around her legs.

There were voices behind the door of her cabin, and for a moment her heart leapt in her chest. Had father awakened? Or had Patrick come to talk to her?

She threw open the door and vaulted through it—right into Josiah Cameron's hulking frame.

"Blast it!" The words sprung from her lips before she had a chance to think. Josiah's hands steadied her, his touch a little too familiar for comfort.

"Aminda Ingerham! Mind your tongue!" Her Aunt scolded. *Could this day get any worse?* "Mr. Cameron has come to inquire of your health. Show him some respect!"

Oh. Yes it could.

"My apologies!" Aminda squawked, pulling away from Josiah in veiled disgust. Ducking her face and hiding her angry blush, she turned to hang her shawl on the hook. Blast Josiah Cameron! The boy was a greasy pest!

She composed her features and faced him. "Thank you, Mr. Cameron, I am well, and you?" The nerve of him sneaking in here when she was out. How dare he? If she had been here alone she wouldn't have allowed him past the door.

Josiah smiled, showing every one of his poorly aligned teeth. His hands were black with soot from the smithy. "Mighty fine, Miss Ingerham," his eyes raked her figure, and his tone implied an answer to a different question. *Ugh.*

Her Aunt smiled conspiratorially. "That's better. I feel I need some air after this stuffy cabin. I'll just leave you two to chat while I step out onto the veranda." She was out the door before Aminda could voice her protest. Wretch of a woman! Were it anyone else, she would be appalled at the thought of leaving Aminda virtually alone with a young man. *Blast.*

Josiah stood there, grinning. Aminda could hardly stand it. He was disgusting. Not trusting her tongue to speak politely, she walked over and pulled a log from the wood box. Her useless aunt had nearly let the fire go out.

"Your Aunt is mighty kind, helping to watch your father so," Josiah said, as if he could read what comment would most annoy her at the moment. Aminda dropped the log on the coals, spraying sparks into the air. She said nothing.

"It's a shame your father lays there so." *Oh, for Mercy's sake.* Would he not shut up? Did he purposely come here to dance on her frayed nerves?

"Josiah Cameron," she said, brushing at the soot on her apron, her back to the fledgling flame. "What is the reason for your visit?" She had tried tact with him before, but bluntness seemed the best course in this instance.

He smiled again, a little less sure of himself, and then reached into his pocket. "My father sent you these," he held a paper parcel just out of her immediate reach. "Nails. Says your father'd bought and paid for 'em, wasn't sure as he needed 'em now, mind you..." he glanced at her father who continued to breathe without consciousness.

Aminda remembered no order for nails from the blacksmith. It was much more likely that Mr. Cameron had sent Josiah to spy. Or Josiah had made the whole thing up to feed his unhealthy infatuation.

Well, he was here, and there was no getting rid of him

until she took the nails.

"Thank you," she said while reaching for the parcel.

Josiah caught her hand and held it. The nails pierced through the package and into her flesh. She yanked back, but he held firm. His eyes were flint and his arm was strong.

"Some say as your father was cursed. Some say as he was caught up in doings he shouldn'ta been. Evil things," he said, low enough that her aunt wouldn't hear. "The village is talking. A woman such as yourself needs a man around. A protector..." he reached up and brushed her cheek with his calloused mitt. She cringed, yanking and prying at his fingers with her other hand. "It would be a shame for anything to happen to such a beautiful young thing, the purtiest girl in the village..."

And then, before she realized what was happening, he caught at her hair yanked her forward and kissed her forcefully.

Aminda reacted instantly. Her free hand swung up and slapped him with everything she had. The sound resounded through the cabin.

"Oh! Is everything all right in there?" Aunt Mary's voice called through the closed door.

Josiah dropped her hand and touched his cheek. His eyes shot daggers at Aminda as he called back. "Everything's just fine, Mrs. Morehouse...just the fire snappin'." His smile was more of a grimace now.

The ingrate! The letch! How dare he!

"Just fine..." He walked over and dropped the nails on the table with a crash. Aminda was so angry she couldn't find words vile enough to throw at him.

He made as if to leave but stopped beside her, leaning in to whisper into her ear. Aminda stood with clenched fists, the reek of his breath nearly choking her.

"I know about the map," he said.

Before she could say anything more, he was gone.

Aminda rushed to the water bucket and scooped up a drink. She gulped it down, rinsed her mouth out and spat into the fire. That rotten beast! She never wanted to be in the same room with that filthy scoundrel again! She snatched for a cloth and scrubbed at her face, scouring every last inch of her cheeks.

Of course it was then that her Aunt Mary chose to enter and say the most outrageous thing Aminda had ever heard. "My, what a fine young man Josiah Cameron has turned out to be. So tall! So strong!"

Aminda spat into the fire again in disgust.

"Josiah Cameron is a filthy beast!" she growled at her shocked aunt.

"Aminda Jane! What has gotten into you?"

"To me? What has gotten into me? Oh, let me think...my father is lying there dying from a mysterious illness, the men are restless at the mill, if father doesn't rouse I may have to sell the only livelihood he has, and your 'fine young man' is...is...a—and he just—" Aminda stopped short. She didn't need more gossip rolling about this ridiculous village.

"And he just what?" her aunt demanded.

Aminda took a deep breath, biting back the curse words she wished to spray at her meddling ninny of an aunt. "And he is not the sort of man I wish to associate with."

Aunt Mary huffed.

"Mark my words, young miss. There may come a day when a strong young man like Josiah Cameron will be the saving of you. You've gotten far too high and mighty for your own good."

She grabbed her bonnet from the rocking chair. "I won't be back if I'm to be treated so. I'll send one of the children to watch your wretched father at noon." She stomped across the floor with her workbasket and bustled out the door, slamming it behind her.

Aminda turned to her father, the noise still vibrating in her ears. He didn't stir.

She stumbled to the rocking chair, fell into it and stared at the darkening coals. Her face burned with anger, disgust and frustration.

And then the vision came.

⁓⦿⦿⦿⁓

Fog and flames swirled around her. A small single-masted sloop slid silently across a river, one man standing tall at the prow. His hair was long and white, as was his beard. His long coat billowed in the breeze. A black flag flew from the mast.

The man was angry. He was gesturing to another man, demanding, arguing. Aminda could not hear what was said but she was sure the second man was frightened. There was a flash and then the second man fell backwards into the river, dead.

The white-bearded man smiled wickedly and then pulled something from his coat before taking the helm. He unfolded it carefully, like a lover's letter. The vision expanded to show the writing on the parchment.

The shock of recognition roused Aminda from her trance. She sputtered and grasped at her pocket. The rustle there reassured her and frightened her at the same time. The murderous, white-bearded man had held the treasure map.

⁓⦿⦿⦿⁓

Aminda sat in front of the coals for a long time. Her head ached from the vision and the stress of the morning. What

21

had her father dragged her into? Was the man in her vision the Whitebeard her father mumbled about in his sleep? Why had he killed the man on the river?

She pulled the map from her pocket and stared at it in the gloom. She recognized the stream and the small bay it opened into, its twists and turns visible from the dam she walked across daily. The next bay down looked like one she had rowed to with her father mere weeks ago to fish. There was a dotted line along the shore and several roughly drawn trees then the number 9, the letter W and a large X.

A treasure map indeed.

Aminda glanced nervously at the door before walking to it and locking the bolt. Perhaps it was time to take precautions. Her father had warned her about a man with a white beard and she didn't doubt she had this man's map.

Hoping her visions were done for the day, she added some kindling to the fire and coaxed it back to life. Blasted Mary, almost letting the fire go out.

And blasted Mary implying that a match with Josiah Cameron was the only one she was capable of making! *Ugh.* She'd rather live her life as a spinster than be tied to that beast. She would be no man's prize. Although the pickings were slim in this tiny village, she loved her stream and her father too much to suggest they move—so she hoped Josiah would fix his desires on some other poor woman.

Her mind whirled through her predicament as she tidied the cabin and swept the floor. She was so absorbed in her thoughts that she jumped when a timid knock sounded at the door.

"Yes?" she called, "who is it?"

"Aminda?" a tiny voice answered. "It's Caroline."

Aminda smiled. Leave it to her aunt to send poor little Caroline to do her dirty work. She walked over and lifted the latch. Her young cousin stood there, bonnet askew and mud on her shoes.

"Well hello there, Caroline. How nice to see you. Did your ma send you?"

Caroline looked at her with huge eyes and nodded.

"Uh-huh," she said. "Ma says as I'm to look after Uncle Joe while you're gone." Caroline was barely eleven, and was unlikely to weigh more than four stone soaking wet.

She peeked around Aminda, eyes widening as she saw Aminda's father.

"Is he really only sleeping?" she whispered.

"Yes, Caroline, he really is only sleeping. He won't move, and he's not sick."

"Are you sure he's not...he's not..."

"Dead?" Aminda finished. "No, he's breathing." She reached out for her young cousin's hand. "Come, I'll show you."

Caroline gratefully took Aminda's hand and tiptoed to the bed with her. Aminda reached out and placed her hand on her father's forehead.

"See, his face is warm—but not feverish—like mine." She reached down and touched his chest, feeling the steady thump-thump of her father's heart. "And his heart is beating. He's just asleep."

"Oh," Caroline said, not sounding convinced.

"And look, Turtle isn't afraid," Aminda said. The cat was curled up near her father's feet.

That settled it. Caroline loved Turtle. She loved her uncle too, but this was not the uncle she remembered. Aminda settled her near the fire with a good book and grasped the keys, warning Caroline to lock the door while she was gone, just in case.

The noon meal passed without incident. And then

Caroline returned again for quitting time. Thankfully the rain had stopped and the sun was breaking through as Aminda rushed down the path to lock the mill for the night. The men waited, took their pay and their dram and strolled away, pipe smoke trailing behind them. Mr. Stairs stood just inside the door, waiting.

"Good evening Miss Ingerham," he said kindly.

"Good evening, Mr. Stairs," she replied. "Anything to report?"

"Naught but the tallies. The usual. Four hundred board feet of lumber drying in the stacks. Jim Jones was a cantankerous old coot today, but he worked as hard as the others."

"I see," Aminda said as she checked the sluice gate and the gears. They were all greased and ready for tomorrow's work. Mr. Stairs did his work well.

"Thank you Mr. Stairs," she said. "And thank you...for your help while father is ill."

He nodded. "Men who are afraid and ignorant are dangerous men. I wish I could do more," he said quietly.

"Well thank you, just the same."

Mr. Stairs lit his pipe as Aminda turned the key in the lock.

"Tomorrow then?" he asked.

"Tomorrow," she replied, and they walked their separate ways.

ᴄᴀᴏᴄᴀᴏ

Aminda walked her young cousin home and hurried along the darkening road to the cabin. The rain had stayed away and the sun was now sinking quickly behind the trees. She wished she had more daylight. The O'Brien's west pasture was too far to walk to in the dark, and she had no wish to be outside when the sun was gone. If only Patrick would chance by.

Aminda did the chores as quickly as she dared, finishing just as the sun disappeared for the night. The chickens squawked their displeasure when she closed them in their coop and Shadow shifted nervously in his stall, which was odd. As Aminda slopped back through the mucky barnyard she recognized the reason why, letting out a barely disguised curse as she did so. Josiah Cameron was leaning on the veranda support, paring his nails with a knife.

Would this day never end? Would the scum not leave her be?

He leered annoyingly as she approached and clumsily slipped the knife into the sheath on his belt.

She glared back at him and made to pass by. His blackened fingers shot out and clasped her arm, twisting her to face him.

"I believe we have unfinished business, Miss Aminda," he said. His breath reeked of rum. "You were about t' beg me t' help you...And your aunt's not aroun' t' interrupt ush now, is she?"

"Get your filthy hand off of me," Aminda said through clenched teeth.

"Or what?" he laughed. "Who's going t' stop me?" He swayed as his free hand gestured to the quiet expanse of trees beyond the barnyard.

"I am," said a deep, strong voice from below the cabin.

Josiah swung around to locate the voice, overbalanced in his drunkenness, and fell off the veranda into the muck.

Patrick O'Brien walked up the path. The legs of his trousers were filthy but Aminda hardly cared. "Are you all right?" he asked. "Sorry you had to deal with that."

He looked down at Josiah in disgust. Josiah flailed about, spitting and cursing. His attempts to wipe his face only made matters worse.

"I suggest you go elsewhere, Josiah...and dry out."

Josiah rolled onto his hands and knees and struggled to his feet. He barely managed the two steps to the edge of the veranda, spewing profanity.

"I didn't ask for your advice, you filthy mick," he said between curse words.

"I'm not the one with grass in my mouth," Patrick said with a smile.

Josiah took a swing at Patrick but Patrick easily stepped out of the way. Josiah landed face-first in the dirt once again.

Aminda stifled a giggle.

Patrick looked up, humour lighting his eyes.

"Perhaps I shall walk Mr. Cameron home. Will you be all right?"

Aminda didn't want him to leave. He made her feel...safe.

"I suppose I shall," she said. She would be fine in the cabin with the door locked...but it would be so much nicer with someone to talk to. The prospect of another long, dark night alone with her half-dead father and the call of the flame was not desirable in the least. Not to mention that when Josiah sobered up he would be angry as hell, and likely to come back.

Josiah continued to sputter, oblivious to the two behind him. He had made it back onto his hands and knees and they both watched as he fought to stand upright. It was like a bad stage comedy. Patrick glanced at her, one side of his mouth turned up in a quirky half-smile.

"I'll come back," Patrick said. "If you'd like."

"Yes!" Aminda blurted out. She caught her breath, realizing how bad that must have sounded. "I would like that," she said more sedately. "It's been a long day."

He tipped his hat and nodded. The look he gave her

awakened something deep in her belly.

"Aye, I'm sure it has," he murmured.

The something in her belly gave a little lurch.

He reached down and grasped Josiah's arm, pulling him upright. Josiah continued to mutter and curse about micks and damned Catholics, but the fight had gone out of him. Patrick grasped him under the arm and half-walked, half-pulled him down the path to the stream and the dam below. He shot her a look and a brief wave as he rounded the corner and walked out of sight.

Aminda sighed and opened the door.

Her father had not moved, but he seemed to have gained a bit of color. She rushed about, doing the chores and heating the last of the stew for a brief meal. The bread crock was almost empty, so she set a new batch by the hearth to rise. Tomorrow she would have to bake on top of everything else.

She carefully fed her father some stew, bathed him, fluffed his pillow, rolled him to a new position and moved his arms and legs a bit to get his blood flowing. Patrick did not come.

She chopped kindling, brought in wood, swept the floor and put down milk for the cat. Still, Patrick did not come.

The dim light in the small cabin window dwindled to blackness. Aminda lit a precious candle and set the kettle to boil. Some tea to settle her nerves—that would do the trick.

Turtle came and rubbed against her legs as she sipped her tea.

"Hello, Turt." Aminda reached down and scratched the cat's ears. He purred and leapt up on her lap, kneading her legs with his paws.

Aminda tried not to think about Patrick, but it was impossible. With the chores done and the light too dim to do needlework, she sat in her mother's rocking chair and rocked with her back to the fire, patting Turtle and sipping tea. There was nothing else to do but think.

The boy was handsome; there was no doubt about that. Dark hair with a glint of red at the sides, blue eyes, tanned skin with a sprinkling of freckles...and he was much taller than most of the young men around here. His quiet intelligence was soothing in a village of hot-headed fools. Although life was hard here in this half-wilderness, it had been harder for the O'Briens than most... and Patrick had taken the brunt of it. She filed through her memory, seeing Patrick at the general store counting pennies for a hoe, bending in the fields behind the plough, shouldering sacks of grain to the grist mill, tipping his hat and giving her a subtle smile as he slipped out of the school door.

She had been haughty and indifferent, the only child of a relatively wealthy man high on her horse looking down at him. Why had she been that way?

A knock at the door frightened Aminda from her reverie and she dropped her tea cup. It smashed on the stone hearth and Turtle flew from her lap, scratching her arm deep enough to draw blood.

"Blasted cat!" she hissed.

"Aminda?" The door shook but the lock held. "Aminda!"

"Patrick!" Aminda hastened to the door and unlocked it. Patrick rushed in. His eye was swollen shut, his cheek bloody.

"Are you all right?" they asked each other in unison.

Aminda blushed and looked down. Patrick covered his eye with his hand.

"Oh," she said. "Your knock startled me and my cat as well." She gestured to her bloody arm. The cat sat on the stairs, cleaning his paws and looking indignant.

Patrick walked a few more steps in. "Do you want me to look at that scratch?" He offered.

She giggled. "I think you need my help more than I need

yours. What happened to your eye? Did Josiah revive?"

He grinned sheepishly. "Not Josiah. His father. Seems hit first, ask questions later is family tradition."

"Oh." The apple didn't fall far from the tree.

Aminda gestured to the table. "Please, sit down. I'll get some water to clean that cut. Would you like some tea?"

She bustled about, drawing fresh water from the well, gathering clean cloths and pouring tea.

"Why would Mr. Cameron hit you?" she asked as she did so. "You were bringing his drunken ingrate of a son home." The memory of Josiah's hand on her arm made her shiver.

"Ah, yes, I was. But it seems Mr. Cameron's view of his son is a bit biased. I suppose he thought it was I who had poured the rum down Josiah's throat. Regardless, I didn't stick around to find out. The man is huge."

Aminda nodded. She dipped a cloth in cool water and lifted it to Patrick's face. "This might sting a little," she said. He flinched as she dabbed the small cut on his cheek.

"Josiah was here earlier today," she said as she gently patted the bruised skin.

Patrick raised his eyebrows in question, cringing as the movement pulled on his cut. "Was he, now?" he said.

"Yes. He was."

Aminda gestured toward the parcel lying on the small table by the door. "He said he was delivering nails that my father had ordered. Which father hadn't."

"I see," said Patrick.

"And then he accused my father of being cursed. Sound familiar?" she said, eyes sharp.

"Aye, it does."

"And then he kissed me without permission, and I slapped him," she said all in a rush.

Now why in Mercy's name did she tell him that? Appalled

29

with herself, she dropped the cloth in the bucket, stood up quickly and marched over to the fire. She distractedly began gathering up fragments of her smashed teacup. Patrick said nothing.

In her haste, her fingers slipped and a piece of china slit her palm.

"Blast it!" she said, and burst into tears.

Behind her, Patrick's chair scraped on the wooden floor. The floorboards shifted and creaked as he knelt down beside her. She felt his hands on her shoulders, gently tugging her toward him. It felt so good to be touched—touched with compassion not violence. She leaned into him and he stroked her hair like she was a child.

"Josiah Cameron is a vicious eejit," Patrick said when her tears had abated somewhat. "I hope you hit him hard."

Aminda smiled. "Hard enough." She sniffed and sat up. There was a large wet patch on Patrick's shoulder, beside several small smears of mud. "Sorry about your shirt."

Patrick shrugged and dug in his pocket for a handkerchief. "My shirt will do. Wish I would have seen Josiah's face when you thumped him. Serves the nasty bugger right."

Aminda smiled. "My aunt didn't think so." She looked down and fiddled with Patrick's hankie.

His eyes widened at that. "Your aunt was here? And she let him..." he stopped at the word 'kiss', "do that?"

"She wasn't in the cabin—had made some excuse about going out for air. She didn't see it happen, and I certainly wasn't going to tell her about it. I might have cursed at him a bit. She didn't like that either."

"No...really?"

"Mmm-hmm. I did."

"Aminda Ingerham, you are a woman of many talents."

Aminda grinned. "You don't know the half of it."

Her hand throbbed and she looked down to assess the damage. It was just a small cut, but blood dripped onto her apron.

"Here. My turn," he said. He hopped up and grabbed one of the cloths from the table, kneeling down before her. More gently than his large hands suggested possible, he grasped her hand with his and dabbed at the cut. When he was satisfied it was clean, he ripped a small strip from the rag and tied it around her palm, closing her fingers over the bandage with his own. He didn't let go.

"There. Keep pressure on it for a while longer. It's not deep."

"Thank you," she whispered.

He smelled of pine and earth. The something in her tummy jumped and squirmed at the pressure of his hands on hers. His thumb shifted, a brief whisper of a caress. Their eyes met and the space between them seemed to hum. Aminda somehow forgot how to breathe.

He dropped her hands and jumped up.

"I should leave. Mother will be wondering where I am," he said, looking away.

She stood up and brushed at her apron. "Yes, I suppose you should," she said, but thought something else.

Patrick walked to the door, and she followed. As he reached for the latch, he turned and faced her.

"Aminda, if I may be so bold..." He reached into his pocket and pulled out a cloth wrapped parcel. "I brought you this." He pushed it towards her. "Here. Take it."

Curious, Aminda took it. The parcel was long and thin.

"It's my grandda's hunting knife," Patrick said, before she could unwrap it. "He died on the voyage across the Atlantic. I'd like you to have it. Josiah may not be the only one to come this way intending violence on the lumberman's daughter."

His eyes were hard and serious.

"I can't take this." She tried to put it back in his hands but he refused to take it back.

"No. It's for you. Consider it a gift of...friendship." The corner of his mouth quirked up.

"But..."

He held his finger up. "I willna take it back." The finger caught her chin and tilted it upwards. "Such beauty...is worth protecting."

He dropped his hand before she could reply and stepped out into the black night.

Aminda sat for a long time by the fire with Patrick's knife on her lap, not caring whether she faced in or out. Today she had been attacked, insulted, threatened and harassed... yet all of that seemed to fade in the light of the gift on her lap and the memory of Patrick's touch.

But what was she thinking? Her father was lying there half-dead. If he were awake he would lock her up for good knowing she'd been practically alone in the cabin with a boy. Not just any boy, either... an Irish Catholic boy. It was just short of cavorting with the devil. Mind you, she'd been alone in the cabin with Josiah Cameron today too, with her meddling aunt's blessing. She didn't think her father would like that either.

She sighed and pulled the tattered map from her pocket. It looked so innocent—a few scribbles and symbols on a piece of parchment. How had her father found it? She held it up to the firelight, searching for clues, watermarks, anything to help her figure out what it meant. Why would someone kill for such a thing? And who was the white-bearded man?

She had avoided her visions for years, why would she have one now? What if she tried to channel the visions? Would she see what she wanted to see? The gypsies did it. They could see your future. They could see things about you if they tried. Was her 'sight' like that? Aminda's mind whirled with questions.

Well, she certainly didn't want to try to have a vision in the dead of night—who knew what she would see. She had had enough excitement for one day. She tucked away the map and the knife, banked the fire, kissed her father and double checked the door before climbing to her loft for the night.

CHAPTER 3

THE WHITE-BEARDED MAN

THE NEXT DAY STARTED OUT much the same as the day before, except for the weather. It dawned clear and warm, a perfect spring day. Aminda did her chores, put the bread in to bake and waited, facing away from the fire, to see if anyone would come today.

Aunt Mary had obviously seen duty as more important than ruffled feathers as it was she, not Caroline, who came to watch her father as Aminda opened the mill.

The weather had also lightened the mood of the men. They were less aggressive, but no less vulgar—joking about things that were not appropriate for mixed company. Mr. Stairs at least had the decency to look embarrassed. Aminda didn't mind. She had spent her whole life around mills.

She did glean one useful tidbit of information from their banter. The tinkers had come into town during the night. They were set up near the agricultural barn in the centre of the village. Aminda needed some tin candlestick holders and baking items so she'd been waiting for their springtime visit. After the noon break she set off with a pocket full of change to make some purchases.

The twenty minutes it took to walk into town was peaceful and refreshing. It was good to be out of the stuffy cabin. Aminda hummed as she walked, eager to spend her clinking coins. The tinkers' wagons were so interesting and brightly coloured that Aminda wasn't paying attention to the tinkers themselves as she approached. When she rounded the first wagon she narrowly missed running into a tall man with a very white beard.

She stepped back in surprise. It was him. The man from the vision.

"I'm sorry," the Whitebeard said with a calm, quiet voice. "I didn't intend to startle you." He smiled kindly.

Aminda was struck dumb. What was the white-bearded man doing here?

He waited politely for her to speak. A sturdy grey pony grazed nearby, munching on the abundant green grass. He stopped and lifted his head as if waiting for her response.

"Uh..." she said stupidly. "I, uh..." *Think, Aminda, think!*

"Can I interest you in some tinware perhaps?" He gestured towards his cart. It was painted bright purple with silver stars and all manner of tin items hung on hooks and portable shelves around him. The pony went back to his grass.

The glint of a small mug brought her out of her stupor.

"Oh, yes... I'm looking for some baking cups, a cake pan... and some candlestick holders..." She peered at him while listing off the items.

His beard was shockingly white as was his hair—the color of fresh snow in the sunlight. He was very tall, at least six feet, and wore a long cloak that was out of style. He looked like a wizard from medieval times. He certainly didn't appear as if he would murder her on the spot.

"Well let's see. Candlestick holders...ah, here we are." He poked through a sack and handed her two simple round

36

holders. "And pans..." He wagged his finger at her. "What size?"

And so it continued until Aminda's arms were full and her pocket was nearly empty. She was very careful not to let him see the map, fighting to cover her fear of him as she did her business. Just as she was handing over the last coins, his hand brushed hers. A shock of visions rolled through her mind and then were gone. The Whitebeard peered over his spectacles at her, a curious expression on his face.

"Have I met you before, Miss?" he asked.

"No," Aminda replied, a bit too quickly. "No, I don't think so."

"Hmmmph." He replied, still eyeing her like a hawk eyes its prey. "Well." He thought for a moment. "Shall I read you your fortune?" He said then, hand outstretched as if to take her own.

"No!" she said. "I mean, no thank you. I don't believe in such things." And she was not going to touch his hand again. Ever.

"Well then. It's been a pleasure doing business with you, Miss." He nodded and turned away to his cart.

Aminda gathered her parcels and fled.

≈≈≈

Later that afternoon Aminda saddled her horse and headed to Patrick O'Brien's west pasture. She felt bad about leaving her father alone again, but he looked so much better it was as if she were leaving to let him have a nap. She locked the door, just in case.

Things had become too complicated for her to manage on her own. The appearance of the white-bearded man had unsettled her, and she needed someone to talk to. No other option seemed available and, truth be told, she wanted to see Patrick again. The 'something' in her stomach was urgent. It was pushing her to do things she never would have done before—namely, visit Patrick O'Brien.

She knew the road to Patrick's farm led from the river road up over the hill. She'd never had cause to take the road, but she'd passed it a few times on the way to Sainte Anne's. It was small and rough, barely passable for a wagon.

Her gelding, Shadow, avoided the worst of the holes and ambled along at a walk up and away from the river. The trees closed in slowly until the road was only a track, and a rough one at that. It was likely Patrick had built it entirely himself, so she refused to pass judgement. After a few minutes she came to a fork in the track. The main path appeared to travel straight ahead. There were two smaller paths, each travelling in opposite directions. At the entrance to the westerly path a hat hung on a tree. It was Patrick's. She swung right and followed it.

Had he left the hat to show her where he was? Maybe it was just a family sign. Either way, she was sure this was where she would find him.

She was right.

After a few minutes in dense forest, she broke free into a muddy field. Long, straight furrows crossed it, dotted with rocks. On the far side a dark head bobbed behind a donkey. The dark head wasn't wearing a shirt. His shoulders were broad, and his hair curled on his forehead where it was stuck with sweat. Aminda's heart did a little flip flop.

He cursed loudly in Gaelic as the donkey planted his feet and the plough jerked to a stop. The donkey brayed and refused to move, straining its head to look at Shadow. Patrick flicked the reins and yelled, but the donkey's braying drowned him out.

Aminda urged Shadow onward, skirting the field toward them as the donkey wrenched his head further and further, finally pulling the plough to the left to get a better view. Patrick threw up his hands in disgust and finally looked to see what was so interesting. He started at the sight of his visitors and then waved a sheepish hello.

"Eee-aw! Eeeee-aw!" the donkey called to Shadow. Shadow stood taller and pranced along the edge of the field.

Trying not to gawp like the village idiot, Aminda pushed Shadow on as Patrick wiped his brow with his shirt and gave another wave. He smiled broadly. She tried to be demure, but found herself beaming back at Patrick. Although the day was merely warm, she had begun to sweat profusely. She likely stank. Her hair was a mess. Her hands were dirty from her chores. She hadn't thought about what she looked like in her haste to just get here.

Patrick nodded as she approached and Aminda tried to keep herself from staring at his bare, tanned chest. She had a million things she wanted to say to him but not one thing came to mind. What in heaven's name was wrong with her?

"I thought you might come," he said when she didn't speak.

She fiddled with her reins.

He waited.

"Would you like some help to get down?" He finally asked.

"Oh!" she said, stupidly. "No, I can get down." She slid down and flipped the reins over Shadow's head. She stood there, struck dumb by the clear view of his chest.

"I hope Josiah hasn't bothered you again."

"Oh, no, he hasn't. I...I just thought you might have a moment. It's been a mad few days, and you'd offered to listen, and I really do need...well, I need someone to talk to. Maybe to tell me I'm not going crazy. I just...It's just..." She stopped and took a deep breath. What was wrong with her? She was dangerously close to crying. What was it about him that made her so volatile? She looked up and met his concerned gaze and then down at the chain and medallion around his neck.

"You're not going crazy," he said.

She laughed.

"Well, that's one good thing," she said.

"And I'd be happy to listen."

"Well, that's another..."

He gestured to the shade by the trees. There was a small log there with a pail sitting beside it.

"How about we sit down?" he said.

Grateful for something to do, Aminda loosely tied Shadow to a tree. She sat on the log while Patrick scooped some water from the pail. It was an awfully small log.

"Would you like a drink?" Patrick asked.

Aminda's throat was dry. A drink would help.

"Yes, please."

She took a drink and slid over as far as she could to give him space on the log. As she did so the water chose a different route. She choked, spewing water and just managing to cover her mouth. Water flew everywhere—down the front of her bodice, on the ground and even out her nose. So much for propriety. She coughed and spluttered and hacked, mortified.

"Are you all right? Can I help?"

Cough, hack, splutter.

"Aminda?" Patrick pulled a handkerchief from his pocket. The second one she'd been offered in as many days. Aminda shook her head, coughing afresh.

Cough, cough, hack. He offered the handkerchief again. When she didn't acknowledge, he began dabbing at the wetness on her dress. Without thinking he rubbed at her breast, realized what he was doing, threw the handkerchief down, stood up and turned as red as his tanned skin would allow. He ran his fingers violently back and forth through his hair, making it stand up everywhere. His mouth opened and closed like a fish as he searched for something to say.

The result was so comical that Aminda's coughing turned to strangled giggles.

"I'm so sorry! Please, forgive me!" He said, running his hands once more through his porcupine-quill hair.

Aminda managed a quick breath.

"It's no problem," she squeaked. "Really! It's fine."

Patrick looked distraught.

"No, really, Patrick. It's okay."

It took five minutes to assure him that her dignity was preserved and that helping her dry off had not offended her in any way. Finally he sat down, though not on the log. He sat on the ground, picking a piece of pink clover and pulling at the florets.

They sat silently, watching Shadow drag at his reins in search of grass. Aminda kept glancing at her companion and at his bare back. It was fine and muscled with the barest sprinkling of freckles.

"Patrick?" Aminda finally got the nerve to speak. "Where did you live in Ireland? Before you came here, I mean."

He looked at her with a question in his eyes. "In Wicklow," he said. "Near Dublin." He looked off at the field, lost in thought.

"Why did you leave?"

"Da was a merchant of sorts. Business went bad. The redcoats came and threatened to lock him up... so we left. He was never one to leave the drink, my da," he said, matter of fact. "But Ma was smart. Had kept a stash hidden, for emergencies, like. We managed passage."

He stopped and picked another head of clover.

Aminda had not known any of this.

41

"So we came to Halifax, then moved again. The money is gone now. But we'll get by." He nodded, as if by him saying it, it would come to pass.

"You work very hard," Aminda said, suddenly sorry she had asked.

"Aye, I do. But it was Ma's brains that got us here. And God's will."

He smiled up at her. "And you? Why did your father choose Kingsclear?"

"I'm not really sure," she replied. "We left Connecticut suddenly. My father was Loyalist to the core, my mother too." She stopped. Talking about her mother was not allowed. It hurt too much.

"Father had always been a lumber man. He needed a stream to dam and a river to sail the lumber out on. This fit the bill, I guess."

Patrick nodded.

"My father didn't choose this place," he said. "I did."

That got her attention.

"You did? Really?"

"Yes, it was me."

"Then why here?"

"It seemed as good a place as any. Land. Trees to build with. Water to sail on. And the stories."

That really got her attention.

"The stories?"

"Aye. The stories. Pirates and buried treasure. The ship across was awash with rumour and tale. Mostly men bored with the monotony, talking the way men will talk. They say that somewhere along the river lies a fortune. In gold." He threw the crumpled bits of clover towards the ground, frightening a chickadee in a nearby bush. "But that's all they are. Stories. Still, a man can dream."

Aminda laid her hand over her pocket. Somehow this wasn't going at all as she had expected.

"I have heard the rumours concerning your father, Aminda," he said, disturbing her even more.

He watched her as he spoke. His voice was barely a whisper. "But I wouldn't use them as others would. Perhaps...perhaps the answer to your father's illness lies within the rumours."

Aminda's heart raced, but not because of his shirtless chest. Did he really know how to help her?

"Do you know how to help him? Is it...possible to help him?" she asked.

"I don't know."

Aminda swallowed, ungraciously.

"He is not sick," she said. "He sleeps. He swallows food. He has no fever."

"What do you think causes it?" he asked.

"I think he is cursed," she said.

Relief washed over her—and a shiver. It was the first time she had spoken her fear aloud. Patrick's eyes were so intensely blue as he watched her.

"A curse is a fearful thing. What makes you think so?"

She could tell him the rest. Or could she? Could she tell anyone?

She put her hand to her pocket and drew out the source of her problems.

"Because of this." And she handed him the map.

Patrick sat for a long time looking at the map without unfolding it. It was amazing how such a little thing could be the root of so much trouble. Aminda suspected he knew what it was. He looked up at her, eyes questioning.

"Go ahead. Open it," she said.

The parchment crackled as he unfolded it.

Aminda looked over his shoulder at the markings on the

43

page. The streams and rivers were there. The number nine, the W, and the X. Of course it was a treasure map—what else could it be?

"My father held the map in his hand the night he...slept. He left without telling me where he was going, with men I didn't know. He came back several hours later, ranting and raving. Then he collapsed...and woke no more."

Patrick surprised her by putting his hand in his own pocket and pulling out a paper himself. He handed it to her.

She unfolded it, curious as to what it had to do with her predicament. It was a press-printed sheet:

Wanted: Information with regards to the disappearances of the following men:
James T. Brown, of King Street
Joseph L. Peabody, of Saint John
Samson R. Smith of Bridge Road
William B. Chalmers, of Main Street
Last seen the eighth of May, The year of our Lord Eighteen hundred and nineteen in Sainte Anne's.
Please contact...

<hr />

Aminda stopped reading. Four men, all disappeared on the same night as her father's curse, all from near Kingsclear. Four men had left with her father that night. She was sure of it. She hadn't recognized them in the darkness—but these names were vaguely familiar.

"They disappeared on the same night," Aminda said.

"Yes. And I'm sure I'm not the only one who has seen this sheet. Nor am I the only one to have put two and two together."

A twinge of fear settled beneath her ribs.

"But..."

She had to think. Where had the men gone? Why hadn't they returned home like her father had?

"Patrick, there's something else," she said. "Twice since my father returned he has woken up—just enough to say a few words—before falling unconscious again. Both times he has said the same thing."

"Yes?"

"Beware the white-bearded man," she said, then stopped and took a deep breath. Patrick was leaning towards her now, and his shoulder brushed her knee. The contact was almost as disturbing as the topic of conversation but in a much more visceral way.

"At first I didn't know who he meant. But now I think I do. And I think he's in the village. Right now."

Patrick listened, eyes thoughtful, as she relayed her visit with the tinker. He asked no questions, and believed her without further explanation. Her visions remained her secret.

"He seemed to know me, but I swear I've not seen him before. Could he have seen my Father that night?"

"I don't know."

Aminda twiddled with the items in her pocket. Her father's watch banged against her finger.

"Oh! The time!" she said suddenly, jumping up from the log. She pulled out the watch and checked it, realizing she had barely enough time to get back to the cabin before Aunt Mary returned.

"I've got to go!"

As much as she wanted to stay, it wouldn't do to be late for Mary's visit. Patrick promised her he would come for a visit, maybe even that night. She mounted on Shadow's back, said her goodbyes and trotted quickly down the sun-sprinkled path from Patrick's field. She was grateful for his promise. He made her crazy life bearable. He didn't question her theory... and he was disturbingly handsome.

She smiled as she reached the road, remembering his flustered dabbings at her breast. Her dress had dried quickly in the spring sunshine so Mary would have no extra reason to bully her. No, she would not let dislike of her aunt dampen her refreshed spirits. Patrick would help her, she was sure of it. He might visit tonight. This thought locked securely in her mind, she gave Shadow his head and cantered home.

Her father's watch had been right. She had just sat down in the rocking chair by the newly kindled fire when her aunt bustled through the door.

"Hmmmph," was all she said.

"Lovely day today," Aminda said, trying to appear as if she had spent the last few hours doing housework and dutifully watching over her poor father.

"Yes, but it looks like rain," her aunt said with a sour grimace.

Well, be that way if you'd like. Wretched woman.

"You'd best be going," Aunt Mary said snootily.

Aminda knew when she was being dismissed. Not that she cared. Her father was fine and she had no desire to stay in the stuffy cabin with the Queen of Crabby.

"I'll be back at half past," she said, and escaped out the door.

Closing up the mill took little time. The men accepted their dram and walked off, slightly less sober, but congenial. Aminda checked that the water wheel was locked, the sluice gates were closed all the way, and that the pins were still firmly in their places. She brought the tallow pot to heat for morning, locked the door and walked back to the cabin. She'd taken to looking around herself as she walked. Between Josiah

46

and the Whitebeard, Patrick's knife was a huge comfort.

Her aunt was still at her customary place by the dying fire and her father still lay silently on his bed. Mary didn't even bother making conversation—she simply packed her basket and left.

Aminda was voraciously hungry. She spent the next half hour at the table peeling potatoes, fetching water and preparing something of a supper. This morning's bread was still fresh, if a little doughy. There were still preserves from last year and a bit of butter for the bread. It was no Sunday roast, but it would do. Turtle rubbed against her legs as she sat alone, eating her simple meal.

Her father swallowed his soupy potatoes. He had lost his pinched look, but other than the reflexive swallowing, did not respond to her coaxing. It was hard to see her father so. He had always been the rock in her world. He had such a physical presence that people looked to him for guidance, but his intelligence, kindness and common sense were his true leadership qualities.

Why had he been so foolish as to get caught up in all of this? And who were the men he had joined? Their names danced just beyond recognition...other Loyalists perhaps?

"What have you done, father?" she whispered to unhearing ears. Turtle hopped up and kneaded her father's bedding, settling down just beside his head. The cat purred loudly, as if to say that he was in charge and nothing would happen while Turtle the cat was on watch.

The cat's dignified air disappeared with a knock on the door. He shot up the loft stairs without a second glance.

"Coward," Aminda said. Her heart was pounding double-time both from the sudden noise and the possibility that Patrick could be outside.

She stopped and took a deep breath, her cheek pressed

to the door.

"Who is it?" she called.

"Finn McKeen, at your service."

The voice was vaguely familiar, but Aminda didn't recognize the name. It was not a time to be opening her door to strangers, especially with the daylight fading fast. She was caught.

"Might I ask your business here, Mr. McKeen?"

"Certainly," he answered back through the narrow wooden door. "I wish to speak with you about your father's illness. I may be able to assist you in restoring him to health."

Seriously? He wanted to help her? Aminda was immediately suspicious. If he knew how to help her father, he knew about the curse—or whatever it was that held her father in this unnatural sleep.

She stood behind the door, unable to decide what to do. Who knew if this man was dangerous? Was he a lawman from Fredericton? Was he one of the men on Patrick's sheet?

Thankfully, before she was forced to decide between propriety and safety, the silence was broken by another voice on the veranda. Only this time she knew exactly whom the voice belonged to.

Patrick.

His voice was calm and steady.

"May I help you?" he asked, as if he was part of the household. A note of warning lay beneath his question.

"Oh! Pardon me," Finn McKeen said. "Are you Mr. Ingerham's son?"

Patrick paused before answering.

"I am a friend of the family. A *close* friend of the family."

What was it about Mr. McKeen that caused Patrick to behave so? Not for the first time, Aminda wished her father had put a window in the front of the house, not the back.

48

Curiosity won over caution. Aminda opened the door.

Finn McKeen was the white-bearded man.

Aminda stood in the doorway staring at the tinker. Patrick stood beside him, alert and wary.

The Whitebeard looked from Aminda to Patrick and back. "I see," he said. It was as if he had read both of their minds at once, seeing the connection that had developed. Or maybe he saw something else. Whatever it was, the one glance he gave her made Aminda feel more vulnerable than ten of the leering lumbermen could have. Their eyes saw what they wanted to see, whereas the Whitebeard's eyes seemed to see what really was.

Her face flushed hot under his gaze.

"The commonly accepted social grace is to invite a visitor in," he said simply.

Where did a tinker come across such manners? Aminda chose honesty as her best policy. "I'm not sure that I want to."

"There is nothing to fear from an unarmed elderly man," he said with a twinkle in his beady black eyes. "Fear lies in the unknown. Perhaps the information I have will dispel your fears. May I?"

Aminda glanced at Patrick, her eyes questioning. He gave a barely perceptible shrug. The old man was right. He was just that: an old man. How could it hurt to hear what he had to say? Patrick could easily outmuscle him if it came to that.

Aminda nodded briefly, opened the door and walked in, leaving the Whitebeard and Patrick to trail behind her.

The Whitebeard walked in to the cabin and straight to her father's bed. He sat on the chair beside him like he had a right to, and then gently put his hand on her father's cheek. He nodded, reached down and grabbed his wrist, holding it with his fingertips. Another nod, as if confirming something he suspected. He delicately replaced her father's hand on top of the covers. Aminda was surprised by his grace and apparent care.

Patrick walked to the fireplace and crooned to Turtle. The cat sat perched on the stairs, hackles up, eyes on Finn McKeen. When the Whitebeard turned and faced Aminda, Turtle hissed.

"Wise cat," Mr. McKeen said. "I wouldn't trust me either, as I see neither of you do." Patrick stood close to the fire poker, arm poised to react. Aminda's hand was in her pocket, clasping the knife.

"Well, I'm afraid I'm all you have. Your father has been cursed." He said it clear and plain, as if he were describing the colour of the sky. As if people were cursed every day in the village of Kingsclear.

"How do you know?" Aminda asked. "What makes you so sure?" Her hand stayed clasped in her pocket.

"You sound like someone who knows of such things," said Patrick. His eyes were dark.

"That, my young Mr. O'Brien, is true. I do know of such things."

Aminda and Patrick spoke at the same time.

"How do you know my name?"

"How do you know of curses?"

The white bearded man raised his bushy eyebrows. "We are full of questions this evening, aren't we?" he asked.

They both stood still, waiting for answers.

He sighed. "Very well. I shall answer your questions. Firstly, Patrick O'Brien, I know your name because I am a tinker. I travel these parts listening for stories and telling them. I know you are Irish by your accent. I know you are Catholic by your medallion." He nodded towards Patrick's chain. "There are few Irishmen in these parts and even fewer who are openly Catholic. And you look like your father. I did not 'know' your name, but I took an educated guess based on reasoning." He stared at Patrick over his long pointy nose. Patrick shifted his weight from one foot to another under the intense black eyes. Turtle hissed again.

"And as for you, Miss Aminda Ingerham, I know your father is cursed...because I am the one who cursed him."

Three things happened at once. Aminda pulled the knife from her pocket, Patrick grabbed the poker and brandished it like a sword and Turtle leapt from his place on the stairs, hissing all the way. The cat landed on Mr. Ingerham's chest and stood protectively, back arched and teeth bared.

"How dare you," Aminda said through gritted teeth.

"Oh, please don't think it was your father I intended to curse. It was an entirely protective enchantment. Whoever broke my enchantment would either die instantly or be driven to their homes and then collapse into an unending sleep, depending on their intentions, of course. Quite tricky... but very useful in the long run."

"You're stark raving mad!" Patrick said. "You speak as if cursing a man were an everyday occurrence! And killing a man...commonplace!" The poker stayed raised.

"But why my father? What did he do to you?" Aminda asked, furious.

"Ah, well, that's the catch," said Finn. "Your father, I'm afraid, got mixed up with men who were less than desirable acquaintances. They were greedy, ignorant men. Qualities, I believe your father did not share. His intentions were honourable."

"Intentions for what?" she asked. "And how do you know what he wanted in the first place?"

"Hmmm. Have I been unclear? I am a tinker. A traveller. I watch. I listen. And I think it is my turn to ask a few questions."

Aminda did not put away the knife nor did she say anything else to this increasingly annoying man.

"What do you know about your father's dealings on the night he was cursed? Specifically, at what time did he leave? When did he return? And did he say anything before he fell into his cursed sleep?"

Aminda said nothing. This man did not deserve her answers. He was the reason her father had lain as if dead for seven whole days.

"You choose not to answer. But I will tell you this. Your father will not wake until I wake him. And I cannot wake him without the answers you give."

He glanced over at Patrick. "And you, Patrick O'Brien. I would not have thought that a devout Catholic such as yourself would be interested in such dark things as pirate gold and lost treasure. Where do you come into all of this? Is it merely to help a damsel in distress? Or is there more to it than that?"

Patrick stood firm, but his cheeks coloured.

"As I have said, I am a tinker. I can wait all night... for no one cares whither I go and what my employ is but myself. Although I would love some tea if you have it, that is."

How dare he?

Aminda glared across the room. "Of course I have tea. I'm not entirely sure I want to offer it to you. You cursed my father, perhaps dooming any hope I have of a decent life, and now you...you sit there at his bedside demanding tea? Tea? Now?"

The strange old man sat there with his fingers folded, smiling innocently as if he had just commented on the weather.

Aminda could not *believe* the gall of him. But if what he said was true, there was no hope for her father except by helping Finn McKeen.

"Fine. I will make us *all* some tea. And I will answer some of your questions. Some. But I refuse to promise you anything." She had not forgotten her vision—the fear on the man's face and the splash that came afterward were stuck in her brain.

Finn inclined his head. "I suppose that will do for now. There may come a time when your 'promise' is required. But not yet. Mr. O'Brien, are you capable of wielding that utensil properly? I believe the fire needs attention if Miss Ingerham is to make us some tea."

And so Patrick tended the fire and Aminda made tea. She sliced some of the better loaf of bread, and used more of her precious preserves and butter.

Finn McKeen set his teacup down after his first sip. "Ahh. Life is so much better with tea. Now. Where were we? Oh, yes. You were about to answer my questions, Miss Ingerham. Namely, what do you know about the night your father stumbled upon my curse?"

Aminda put the knife back in her pocket and sat down, her back warmed by the fire. She swallowed. How much should she tell him? Certainly not everything.

"I know very little. My father left the house with four men. It was dark, but they had a lantern and I could see there were four others. I knew none of them. He returned before sunrise, agitated and talking madness. Just after he got through the door he collapsed. It was all I could do to get him to his bed. And then he slept... and did not wake."

Finn's beard folded and unfolded as he nodded his head. "Full dark to before sunrise." He continued to nod. "But did he say anything? Speak the truth, Miss, for I will know if you lie."

Aminda remembered his words clearly. But when she spoke, she did not look at Finn McKeen. Her words were only for Patrick. "He said three things. 'You mustn't speak,' 'Go by moonlight'...and,'" she turned to look directly at Finn, her eyes cold. 'Beware the Whitebeard'."

Turtle hissed. Patrick's eyes widened. And Finn McKeen laughed.

"Well, then. Consider yourself warned. Your father is a wise man. I am not to be trifled with. However, you need not be frightened by me now. If I were going to kill you I would have done so long ago. You see, I believe we can help each other. Your father, in setting off the curse, has alerted me to the presence of something I most sincerely desire. And I believe the answer to where it is lies in your pocket."

Aminda flinched, a small movement but enough to confirm Finn's statement. She could have kicked herself. When would she learn to hide her reactions?

Finn raised his eyebrows. "Yes, Miss Ingerham. I see my deductions are correct. May I see it? The map, I mean, not the knife."

Patrick tensed. "No," he said. "Aminda, don't give it to him."

Finn did not move. His beady eyes stayed locked on Aminda's.

Aminda was pinned by his gaze. Like one of those beetles on a card. Stuck. She wanted to move, but couldn't. Just like she felt when...

And then the vision came.

⌒⌒⌒⌒

It started in blackness. The black of the Whitebeard's beady eyes, swirling softly with fog. Then a lantern, yellow light that threw sinister shadows on the walls of a tavern. She peered through a window grimy with soot. Men of all shapes and sizes sat within, drinking and rocking with laughter.

Aminda immediately recognized one of the men as her father.

Finn McKeen sat at a table by himself in the corner. Those who walked by avoided him as if he were diseased, or perhaps they didn't see him in their drunkenness. He gazed at the mug in front of him, tipped the contents into his mouth and then slammed it down on the table empty. A single tear slid from his eye. He reached into his cloak and pulled out a small piece of parchment, unfolded it and set it on the table. The serving wench laid another mug on the table, spilling beer onto the parchment.

Finn snatched it up from the sodden table and shook it, and then wiped it with his cloak sleeve. He grabbed the mug and downed it. Two seconds later his head crashed to the table. The parchment fluttered to the floor.

Aminda watched her father stand, nod to his friends and head towards the door. He stopped mid-stride, noticing the parchment. In a single fluid motion he swooped down and picked it up, casually refolding it and tucking it into his coat, with hardly a glance at where it came from or who it belonged to. And then he walked out the door.

⬥⬥⬥

Aminda gasped.

"Aminda!" Patrick shouted. "Are you okay?"

She looked around herself, disoriented, and then tried to act as if nothing had happened.

Finn McKeen laughed.

"I wondered," he chuckled. "So you have the Sight. That will be very helpful. Tell me, do you see the future as well as the past?"

Aminda blinked, dumbfounded. How did he know?

"I sensed the Sight in you this morning at the market. You

are untrained, but still the Sight will be a boon."

This statement frightened Aminda more than anything the Whitebeard had said so far. The Sight. He had called it the Sight. In Aminda's world the Sight meant witchcraft. And witchcraft was not a thing to be training. Witchcraft meant damnation and burning stakes.

"You're wrong," she said.

"Wrong?" he asked. "About which part? Seeing the past, or that you are untrained?"

"About all of it."

"Aminda Ingerham, I am rarely wrong. And I rarely lie. You, on the other hand, may be guilty of both things."

Aminda felt more and more panicked. How did he know?

"I have watched many people experience a vision. In fact, I have studied the Sight quite intensely. There are three signs of a vision experience: loss of eye focus, decreased respiration and loss of contact with your environment. You demonstrated all three. Gave Mr. O'Brien quite a fright. Of course, I have also studied the induction of the Sight in those who are unaware of their tendencies. But I can tell from your post-vision reaction that you are familiar with your abilities."

"Now. If I am to help your father, I need to know what you saw. Was it a chest? A cave?" he asked like a child lusting over candy.

She had very little choice. He knew how to help her father. But she would have preferred it if Patrick didn't know.

Finn saw her glance at Patrick.

"So, you don't want Mr. O'Brien to know. How charming. Would you like him to leave?"

"No!" She said, a little too quickly. She didn't want to be left alone with a murderer. She turned to Patrick, eyes pleading. "I'd like you to stay. If you want to, that is." *And if you can handle it.*

Patrick nodded, jaw set. "I will not leave you alone with this man. I offered you friendship, and I stand by that offer."

"Very sweet," the Whitebeard said. His eyes were still on Aminda. "You were about to tell me what you saw?"

"Fine. I saw a tavern. You were drunk. My father found a piece of parchment on the floor of the tavern. He picked it up and left."

Finn looked disappointed.

"That was all?"

"Yes. There were many others in the tavern, but I only recognized the two of you."

"So. I always wondered who had taken it. I thought it had been stolen from me. But I see I was just as much at fault."

"But does it mean anything?" she asked.

"Mean anything? Well of course it means something. Your father was not a true thief, merely a participant in a chain of circumstances. That probably protected him from the original curse."

"Oh," Aminda said, clearly not understanding.

"Well. If that is all you saw, then that is all you saw. No use trying to wring water from a rock, although it has been done before..." He stopped, eyes distant. "No matter." He picked up his tea cup. "It is my turn for some telling. If there is more tea, I would appreciate a spot to wet my throat. Mr O'Brien, I am not going to turn into a dragon and devour Miss Ingerham. She is beautiful, but not my type. You may relax."

The tea was still warm. It soothed her rattled nerves and gave her something to focus on. She was too embarrassed to look at Patrick. What did he think of her now? She lit a few candles, consciously looking away from the flame. She hadn't told anyone of the trance the fire brought on until now, and she didn't want anyone to know. Visions, trances, 'the Sight', whatever you called it, it hinted of witchcraft. No self-preserving young woman would advertise such an ability. And it frightened her that the Whitebeard could induce the trance just by staring her down.

Not good. Not good at all.

Patrick watched Aminda carefully, but not unkindly. He had knowledge of such things. There had been an old granny in Ireland that some went to for tea readings and fortune tellings. Her predictions had always been accurate. But in rural Ireland, people merely accepted this as part of life. Women were not burned at the stake for knowing things, at least not by the old Irish.

Things were different here.

The Whitebeard sipped his tea and then cleared his throat.

"Now. I will tell you a story of love, disaster and intrigue. Believe what you choose to or accept it as an old man's ramblings. It is up to you." He glared at them both, a challenge in his eyes, and then he began.

CHAPTER 4

THE WHITEBEARD'S STORY

"IN ORDER TO TELL THE story in its entirety, I must take you back thirty years ago. I was in Ireland. Yes, Ireland, young O'Brien. I travelled as a tinker, but within my cart were many books and many items of study. At the time I was in Galway, I believe. I was close to a discovery, an important discovery. One that could change my life and the lives of many others.

"There was a woman...a beautiful, strong-willed woman..." His eyes went distant, his face wistful. "Such a woman as I had not seen in many, many years. She had beautiful hair the colour of roasting chestnuts. And like you, Miss Ingerham, she had the Sight. We were married, by actions and words, not by a priest, and we lived and travelled together for a year. One day she came to me, her eyes haunted. She had looked into the fire and seen my future. Stupidly, I demanded that she tell it. I should never have asked. She told me, speaking with strong words and a sad voice. She had seen that I would succeed—gain what I most wanted but lose what I needed. Her words confused me. I thought what I wanted most was her. But I was greedy and self-centred. I wanted fame. I wanted fortune. She wanted a simple life, away from prying eyes. I needed her to tame my foolish desires.

We parted ways. My ambition was not hers. I travelled to the edges of the island, studying and experimenting. I turned my love for her, and my grief at her loss, toward knowledge. Lust. Adventure. And at length, my experiments were as successful as she'd told me they would be. It was then that I boarded a ship, bound for the New World with my knowledge. I had gold in my eyes and held gold in my pockets.

"I came to the New World, landed in Halifax, and hid my gold and my knowledge away. The long, harrowing journey across the ocean's abyss had given me far too much time to think. I began to realize my folly in leaving the woman I loved. I was brash, ignorant and careless. I found my solace at the bottom of a bottle.

"My life became meaningless. I had no need for treasure. No desire for money. So I buried the last of my treasure twenty years ago and all but one of my maps and keys with it. I slipped away in the moonlight, sailing south to the Americas and the Caribbean, drunk and penniless. The map was stolen from me on the way, and the drink stole my memory. Only the key remained." He reached down the neck of his cloak and pulled out a small brass key. "I stayed in the islands for years searching for the thief. The north called to me, though, its voice whispering in my dreams.

"Finally, I set off toward the northern shores hoping I could rediscover the treasure on my own. And as fate would have it, the map found me. A ferryman showed it to me on the river. I... took it from him in a frenzy. All that mattered was the map. It is not a moment I am proud of.

"In a relapse of melancholy and self-disgust, I spent one night in a pub. Just one. I drank until I couldn't see straight. Trying to find hope in the bottom of a cup. That night in

Sainte Anne's, the map disappeared from my table. I feared it had been stolen again. But your vision, if correct, has told me that my own stupidity caused me to drop it on the floor.

"You have heard the stories of gold in these parts, though the stories call it pirate gold. True, treasure abounds on the islands and in caves near the Atlantic coast. Gold dug deep into the bottoms of streambeds and forest floors. Most of it is mine, but I want nothing to do with it.

"The only treasure I am interested in is the one that lies near here. A few paces from some rocks in a stream. I hid it well, and set a curse upon it.

"I believe your father met with others who were interested in the treasure, and convinced them to follow him. They knew of the curse. They followed the rules. I suspect they weren't sure about the map, but if they were careful, and observant... they might have found clues I left in my haste many years ago. Clues to the real whereabouts of the treasure were visible, I'm sure, especially if they went at the dark or the light of the moon. Ah, but it is obvious that someone, at some point, broke their silence. The treasure would have gone back to its hidden grave. Your father escaped with his life, but it is likely the others did not.

"And so we come to you, and how you can help me. I need the treasure. More specifically, I need the book hidden within the treasure. The cure for your father's curse can be found within the book. I have no use for the gold, for within the book lies a recipe, or a spell, if you'd like, to turn wooden coins into gold ones. I can make more. If you will help me—with the map, your strength and your secrecy—you may keep the treasure and do with it what you'd like. I believe within this, the last of my treasure troves, lies the maps and the keys to other caches near here. You may keep these too. I only wish to return to Ireland with my book in hopes that the woman I love still lives.

"Will you help me?"

CHAPTER 5

PLANS

THE ROOM WAS SILENT EXCEPT for the slow crackle of the fire and the steady whistle of her father's breathing. Turtle's eyes had closed. He had given up on his hissing and was curled by Mr. Ingerham's head.

The Whitebeard was lost in his tea cup, swirling the contents aimlessly.

Aminda couldn't stand it. "The man on the river. I saw him. You *killed* him for the map. How do I know you will not do the same to me? Or Patrick?"

Finn's black eyes were alert. "You saw it in a vision," he said, matter-of-factly.

"Perhaps," she replied, and waited for his answer.

He thought for a moment.

"You do not know. I may still kill you. But I cannot reach the treasure alone. It is one of the conditions I placed, thinking I would not return without...without help. And you look like someone I once cared for."

He was silent again, twirling his cup.

"As I told you before, I do not often lie. I give you my word that you and Mr. O'Brien will remain safe if you help me and do what I ask, exactly as I ask it. There is still danger involved. You may die. But I swear that it will not be intentionally by my hand. That is all I can give you."

Patrick spoke for the first time. "The word of a murderer is worth nothing." His eyes were dark. Wary.

"Then you may opt out now, Mr. O'Brien. You have no stake in this adventure. You have heard my story, and I suppose even that is too much. If you leave, I may have to kill you to protect my secrets. If you stay, you are included in my promise."

Patrick's eyes did not change. He looked the Whitebeard up and down, as if assessing the danger he posed. Finn McKeen was frail and old. Patrick was young and strong.

Finn saw his glance and laughed. "No, I do not look like much, do I? But even without strength, one can kill. I can kill without a touch, without a sword and without a pistol. I know my strengths and my weaknesses. If I choose to kill you, young O'Brien, you will die." His shoulders broadened and he seemed to grow with this speech, from an elderly man to a towering, dangerous threat. His eyes burned down, testing.

Patrick leaned back unconsciously. The Whitebeard laughed and sunk back, wrinkled and stooped once more.

Aminda did not doubt his abilities.

Patrick glanced at Aminda, considering. He nodded and then faced the Whitebeard. "I accept. I will help you, and in doing so help Miss Ingerham. But I will be watching you, Finn McKeen."

Finn chuckled. "Then you are a wise young man. It is always wise to face the one you trust least. Although I suggest you save some time for the beautiful Miss Ingerham."

He winked at her, then scraped his chair back and stood up faster than his years implied he could.

"The thing must be done in the full or the dark of the moon.

We have eight days. I will return on the day to make plans. In the meantime, I see you have learned the trick to keeping your father alive, Miss Ingerham. Continue to nourish him and he will be fine. Mr. O'Brien, I would also suggest you keep a wary eye out for Mr. Josiah Cameron. I don't like the look of that boy. And do not mention the map. Speaking of which, I believe it is *still* in your pocket. May I see it? Just for now. I'll leave it with you as it will be safer here."

Aminda shrugged and pulled it from her pocket, throwing it on the table with disgust. It had caused her nothing but trouble. She wouldn't care if he took it.

Finn reached out and took the map, carefully unfolding it and spreading it on the table. Patrick leaned in and looked at the markings.

"Do you recognize these places?" Finn asked.

"Aye. I do. The first stream is the one we are on. Two north of us lies the Koac. This one, here." He pointed to the narrow markings on the parchment. "I've fished up this stream, but only in broad daylight. Some say it is haunted."

Finn chuckled. "A few well placed rumours can go a long way. I started those rumours thirty years ago."

He eyed Patrick, and then Aminda. "One thing you must know," he said in a low voice. "This much I do remember: The map is wrong. The treasure is not nine paces from the waterfall at the top of the stream. I placed a dummy chest there. It is cursed as well, to prevent any others from attempting further searches. I will show you where the treasure lies, but only when we reach this place." He stuck a crooked, long-nailed finger down onto the parchment X.

Then with a sweep of his cloak he turned, threw the map on the table and strode toward the door.

"I will return on the eve of the full moon with what supplies are needed. Until then, tell no one of our conversation.

Tend to your father, Aminda," he said, with a surprisingly gentle tone. "He will recover." He smiled at her in an almost grandfatherly way.

"Until the full of the moon," he said, nodded, opened the door and walked into the night.

Aminda and Patrick stood silently, recovering from the Whitebeard's presence. He was a whirlwind. A whirlwind that had given them both much to think about.

Aminda folded the map and stowed it in her pocket, suddenly very aware that she was alone with Patrick O'Brien again. Well, alone if you didn't count her cursed and sleeping father.

But now Patrick knew her secret.

"You don't have to do this, you know," she said, barely audible.

"Aye, I do."

She raised her eyes and met his. He was watching her. He didn't look like he thought she was a freak.

"Does it bother you? The visions part, I mean. I didn't...I didn't tell anyone. Not even my mother knew."

"It's a heavy burden to carry all alone. I suspect there have been other times you have seen things, frightening things. Murders, perhaps."

"No other murders," she said. "But I have seen deaths." It was strangely liberating to tell someone of her ability. It had been a night for strangeness.

"Until tonight, though, I only saw the visions in the fire. I hate fire. For the obvious reasons, of course, but mainly because of the visions. It's staring into the fire that brings them on."

Patrick nodded. "Hence the reason why you face away."

"You noticed that?"

"Aye. I've noticed."

"Oh."

Aminda hadn't thought she was noticeable.

"The Whitebeard was right, you know," Patrick said.

"Right? About which part?" Aminda asked.

"You are beautiful," he said.

Was it hot in the room? Aminda glanced at the fire. It had died down to embers. The candles spluttered on the table. Turtle purred.

Patrick was still watching her.

Her hand went to her throat. She tucked her hair behind her ear.

He walked around the table and stood in front of Aminda. "I should go," he said quietly. "It's late."

"Oh."

It was late. He should go. But she didn't want him to. No, she didn't want him to leave at all.

"I...I am glad you could come, although the evening didn't quite go as expected," she said. She stood up in front of him as if to see him off, trying to decide what she should do with her hands. She fiddled with her hair, patted at her apron... pesky things, hands.

"Aminda," he said.

She looked up. He stepped closer.

He was so tall. The firelight lit up his blue eyes. They shone down at her. And then...he kissed her.

The sensation was so different than with Josiah. With him, everything in her was repulsed. But now, with Patrick, the something in her stomach enveloped her and swallowed her and her head felt light. Her hands found their place on his neck, on his chest. And for the first time in seven days, she felt safe. She wanted to cry. She wanted to laugh.

His lips found her eyelids. Her cheeks.

She moved to kiss his throat. Their noses collided with

a crack.

"Oh! Sorry!" They both said in unison.

Aminda dissolved in a fit of the giggles.

"Aminda! Did I hurt you? Are you all right?" Patrick asked in a somewhat strangled voice.

What had come over her? She wasn't a silly girl like the others at school! Why couldn't she stop giggling?

"...Sorry...!" she managed to get out between snorts. The look on his face was comical.

He stared at her, not knowing what to do.

His lips twitched, first a little, then a lot. He chuckled, reaching out to caress the bridge of her nose. "You have a hard nose, Aminda Ingerham."

And then he kissed her again.

Chapter 6

Unrest

PATRICK LEFT SOON AFTERWARDS. AMINDA stood and watched him disappear through the woods, then closed the door. She was surprised by how badly she had wanted him to stay. It would have been entirely unseemly, but she had wanted it. His kisses still burned on her lips, but the light seemed to have gone out of the evening. The candles flickered, the fire low. She built it up again, and sat in front of it, facing in. Tonight she would let the visions come.

But they didn't. She stared into the fire long and hard, hoping to see something that would cool the fire in her chest. Her father was cursed. She was going to help the man who had cursed him. She might die.

And, she was falling in love.

Emotions stormed around under her ribs with the rising flames. But she saw nothing more than light and smoke and shadows. No murders, no deaths, nothing.

She wondered what lay ahead. Would they find the treasure? Did she even want it? To her, the treasure she needed was her father's cure. And maybe more time with Patrick.

Her stomach fluttered like the flickering heat in front

of her.

She shook her head at herself. She wasn't the sort to get all moony about a boy. Yet his iceberg blue eyes seemed to do something to her, change her. He was so very wrong for her. The villagers would have seizures. But Aminda Ingerham was not one to care what the villagers thought. The fact that she continued to run the mill was proof of that.

When her eyes began to close she gave up searching the flames. Perhaps she had a quota, one vision a day. Who knew?

She was just about to rise when the feeling hit her.

It started with dizziness. Swirling, then a fire-rimmed blackness. Inside the blackness rose a picture.

A man running. Running as if the hounds of hell chased him. Rock walls and darkness surrounded him. His eyes were wide, his skin tight on his forehead. He was terrified.

Aminda watched him run, spellbound. Something evil pursued him. Something large and frightening and deadly—Aminda could feel it through the edges of the vision.

The man tripped and fell, arm outstretched. And then the blackness swallowed him whole.

Aminda gasped and the scene evaporated in the smoke. She hated the visions. They left her feeling cold and filled with fear, yet somehow empty. She didn't know the man but she had felt his fear as if it were her own. To die in such a place, with no one he loved...Aminda shivered.

Enough. It was only a vision. Not real. Not here. No one she knew.

She stood and brushed the vision away with the wrinkles in her skirt.

She checked on her father, moved his legs and arms, kissed him on the forehead and scratched Turtle affectionately under the chin. Then she climbed up the stairs, blew out the candle and fell into sleep before the wick was cold.

Beyond the cabin, in the dark shadows beside the path, a silent figure lurked. His mood was as black as the night sky above and his mind was a pit of anger. He had come to spy on Aminda, perhaps to steal another kiss from her sweet lips. His plans had been thwarted as he watched first the crazy old tinker and then the O'Brien filth climb the path to the Ingerham cabin—a cabin he thought they had no right to be in. Jealousy had drawn him forward to listen. The cabin walls were thin and he had been close enough to hear snippets of their talk.

He knew now that the tinker was more than just a tinker. He had heard enough to burn Aminda Ingerham as a witch. But witch or not, Aminda Ingerham was his. Patrick O'Brien would pay for touching her. It had taken all of Josiah's limited self-control to stay hidden as O'Brien closed the cabin door and walked smugly away. And when the coast was clear, he had fought with the deep desire to break down the cabin door and have his way with Aminda right then and there.

He rubbed absently at his bruised eye, considering that option as he stretched his stiff back and slunk from his hiding place. No one was around; no one would hear her plea for mercy...

No. He would bide his time... he needed to wait until Aminda had the gold. Then he would possess them both and ride away from Kingsclear a rich and satisfied man. He smiled a twisted smile at the thought. Mrs. Aminda Cameron would be an obedient wife. He would make sure of that.

Shadow danced in his stall and whickered a warning as Josiah slithered down the path, slippery as a serpent—but Aminda was already fast asleep.

The next day was Sunday. Aminda awoke to the purring of the cat and the demented screeching of the rooster. She much preferred the cat. He was warm and comfortable beside her leg. The rooster would pick and scratch even if she fed the ungracious twit. Maybe it was time for rooster pie.

As the chores would not do themselves and she had somewhat neglected the farm as of late, today would have to be spent at home rather than with...

Patrick.

Oh.

Last night's madness came crashing back at her. It could have been just a dream. But that would mean that her father's curse, the Whitebeard, the visions...all of it would be a dream. No. It had been real. Now all she had to do was wait until the full moon and things would return to relative normalcy again. Her father would wake up, she could go back to her world of baking, cleaning, helping run the mill and avoiding Josiah Cameron. But that would be so...dull. Except for Patrick He was far from dull. The memory of his kisses lingered on her lips.

It was as if in one night all of the adventure, all of the living that she had ever dreamed of had showed up on her doorstep. No, *smashed* down her doorstep. She had danger. She had intrigue, she had love, she had...magic. It was both exciting and terrifying.

The rooster crowed again.

Idiotic bird. Feed him or wring his neck. Either one would shut him up.

Downstairs nothing had changed. Her father was still cursed. The cows needed to be milked, the chickens needed to be fed and the horses needed hay and water. There were eggs to collect, a garden to weed, bread to bake, butter to churn, wages to tally, washing to soak and grain to grind.

But it was Sunday. Technically speaking, she should only be doing the bare necessities. If she had a normal family, one with a mother, a father and dozens of happy little children running around, Sunday would be spent meditating, reading the Bible and eating cold food in relative silence—that is to say, different from every other day of the week. As it was, Aminda was used to silence. Silence was her middle name. When he wasn't cursed and sleeping like the dead, father puttered outside or at the mill. On Sundays he puttered in the barn, away from prying eyes. No one came up the hill from the mill on Sundays as the mill was shut down for the day. It was a lonely life; the only interruptions were her days at school and trips into the village for items she couldn't make herself. Come to think of it, the schoolmaster demanded silence, so even that was quiet.

She had heard the rumours about her father and his illness. If she didn't make it to morning services it would only feed those rumours. So she would go to the services and listen to the pastor spewing his tales of damnation and hellfire. With her father cursed, the troubling visions, and threats on her life...what did she have to lose?

She worked her way through the early morning. By the time she had to leave for Sunday services, she had most of the chores done and the bread set to rise. Her father had been fed, moved and cleaned. All things considered, he was looking pretty good. Well, except for the cursed part. But he had some colour; he didn't look quite so malnourished, and he was sleeping peacefully, as if he were just having a Sunday morning nap.

She left Turtle in charge, locked the door and slipped

down toward the mill.

Josiah Cameron was waiting on the bridge.

She had no choice but to speak to him as he was blocking her way. She nodded, and said a perfunctory "Mr. Cameron," before attempting to pass. He had a dark bruise under his eye and healing scratches on his nose.

"Miss Ingerham." He slurred the "Miss" insultingly and his eyes raked her figure as he said it.

Aminda refused to rise to the bait. She pushed by, on the upstream side, of course. It was better to fall into a few feet of water than thirty feet of nothingness.

He followed her, walking beside her in big strides. Not for the first time, Aminda cursed her skirts. They swished under her feet, threatening to trip her up if she went any faster.

They walked on. Josiah smirking at some inner joke, Aminda in stony silence.

"Josiah Cameron. What do you want?" she finally said, stopping in the roadway to confront him.

"Oh, I believe you know what I want, Miss Ingerham," he said, the slur even more pronounced.

Aminda thought of a few choice words, but refused to let them out.

"I'll admit I know very little of love and even less about the marital state. But one thing I know for sure, Josiah Cameron, I will never marry someone with whom the two cannot coincide. I do not, nor will I ever love someone who talks to me so. I suggest you find some other lumberman's daughter and attempt to woo her. I wish you the best of luck."

She nodded and rushed off into the little white church just as fast as her skirts would allow her. The first hymn was being sung. People turned and stared as the two of them entered. One or two of the old grandmas gave Aminda a knowing look.

Great. Now everyone thought she was being courted by Josiah Cameron. Well let them think. She smiled back innocently. Unfortunately, arriving late meant that the only seats left were in the middle of the church. One pew with room for two. Barely. Aminda sighed inwardly and slid into it. Josiah slid in beside her, still smirking. His thigh pushed against hers obnoxiously. Something in his pocket jabbed her, but she didn't dare move.

Mrs. Long, on Aminda's other side, shot her a look while she droned piously along. So, the overly endowed woman had hoped to have the empty space to spread out her voluptuous midsection? Too bad for her. Aminda grabbed a hymnal and prayed that the pastor had planned a short sermon.

The hymn went on and on...and on. The congregation sang on diligently, with no connection whatsoever to the words of the hymn. Tired people singing tired notes. Singing of joy in near death tones just seemed wrong. It was the ultimate oxymoron, singing 'joyful, joyful' in between a leering brute of a boy she loathed and a heavyset grump of a woman in a hot, stuffy church, about to listen to the most depressing sermon on the earth while there were so many other things she would rather be doing.

Like pulling her teeth out with a meat hook.

As she had done so many times before, she smiled and nodded, pretending to be oblivious to their stares, pretending to be the obedient fifteen-year-old protestant daughter of a normal, Christian household.

Oh, yes, there were many things she would rather be doing.

And then Pastor Brown began to speak. There were the usual pleasantries, the welcomings and the opening statements. Preaching about the health of one's soul, the importance of regular attendances at services and the like. Aminda felt her mind wandering before he even got going.

But then one word caught her attention. It was all she could do not to widen her eyes and show her fear.

Curse.

"In every society lies a malevolent force. One which feeds and grows underneath the surface. It is nurtured by some. Gossip...Lies...Greed...For-ni-cation..."

He extended the word as if thrilled by it. Aminda imagined he was. The pressure from Josiah's thigh increased.

"Those who nourish evil, at first innocently, find that they are pulled into the blackness below. The devil is not an easy master. Hell's General thirsts for minions! He sends out his commanders searching for souls. He feeds on the weak minded and the low in spirit and makes them his. They become the cursed. Damned! Worshipers of Satan! Enemies of the light!"

His eyes threw sparks as his fist pounded down on the pulpit. Sparks directed at Aminda. She glared back.

"Evil lies in every corner of this land, waiting for those who would fall into its clutches. Even here. Even here! In our small village! Eee-vil—waiting to harvest the souls of our children!" His outstretched finger swept the congregation. A drop of spittle dripped and dotted his chin.

Aminda waited, knowing what was coming next.

"We must fight against the evil in our midst! The Bible tells us "thou shall not suffer a witch to live!" And will we? We must fight for our children! Repent and teach them the teachings of God! Act against the cursed!"

The walls seemed to be closing in on her. Aminda fought to take slow, steadying breaths. Josiah shifted, jamming his thigh against hers. Threatening. Accusing with a touch.

"If we root out this evil, find it and cast it away, we can still save ourselves and our families! There is still hope! We must be warriors in prayer. Pray for the evil doers! Constantly!

Make them see their evil ways! They must repent and be saved from their wickedness. Brought to the eternal light! And we must search out our own transgressions. Cast out the log in our own eyes! We are all to blame for this plague of iniquity! We must fall on our bellies and pray for lenience in the sight of the Almighty! And the Devil's servants must be brought forward and punished!"

He went on and on. Repent. See your wickedness. Sweat ran from his brow and stained the creases of his robe. The air was thick with humidity and the scent of unwashed human. Josiah pushed harder against her leg. She was caught like a rabbit in a trap. Forget the afterlife; she was stuck in her own private purgatory. She held herself as upright and as small as she could, her hips aching from the constant effort. She shifted slightly towards Mrs. Long, and got an elbow in the ribs in return.

Speaking of witches.

Aminda sat and stewed, fighting against the heat of the room. She felt light-headed and concentrated on taking deep, steady breaths. Even sweaty, smelly hot air was better than none.

It was with great relief that she felt Mrs. Long shift to reach the hymnal. The hour-long sermon was a fog of hate, hell and accusation. Aminda was sure she had plenty to repent for, but a devil worshipper she was not. The congregation stood to sing the recessional. Aminda gripped the pew in front of her and innocently shoved back at Josiah, carving out space in the cramped pew.

Before the last droning notes of the hymn had trailed away, Aminda shot behind Josiah and into the aisle. She was the first one to shake the pastor's hand, smiling innocently the whole time, and the first one out of the church. Josiah, as she had hoped, was stuck in the throng. She had to hold herself back from running down the walkway. People talked about her enough.

The fresh air helped clear her foggy brain. She didn't look back. She didn't want to waste time. Unfortunately, she wasn't fast enough.

"You should be honoured to be seen walking into services with me. A fine, young protestant man is what you need," he said as his footsteps echoed behind her.

She cringed. Was he thick in the head? Didn't he see how much she hated him? How little she cared for his chauvinistic opinion? He was not fine, and she would never be honoured to be seen with him. He looked like a pirate with his bruises and scrapes.

"Alice Joslin practically falls at my feet when I walk by her."

Aminda chose the silent approach. Her mind whirled. How could she get rid of him before she got home?

"Not a bad kiss that one. And she lets me touch her—"

"*Mister* Cameron! Do you mind? I have absolutely no interest in what you and Alice Joslin have been up to!"

So much for the silent treatment.

He sneered down at her. "A bit prudish are we? That's quite all right with me. I like my women to have a bit of decency."

She stopped. He had an infuriating ability to get under her skin. She was sure her face was beet red and blotchy. The sun was hot and the breeze could only do so much to diffuse.

"Mr. Cameron. I have absolutely no interest in you, nor do I want to hear about what you do or do not like in 'your women'. I have no intention of ever becoming one of them."

"Oh, I think you do."

Aaargh! Was he deaf? Or insane?

"No, I don't. And no threat of yours will change my mind."

"What was Patrick O'Brien doing at your house last night?

I saw him leave. Late. You wouldn't want the village to think you're entertaining young men late at night. Young Catholic micks. Spreading your legs to the scum of the earth. Word gets out, you may find you have a line-up at your door."

So this was his new attempt at blackmail.

She shook her head and continued to walk. "Go ahead and ruin what little reputation I have, Josiah. I am not afraid of you. In fifteen years I have never given any indication of such wantonness. Patrick O'Brien is a friend. That is all. I have a mill to run, a farm to manage and a sick father to tend. He offered his help. Nothing more. Perhaps you could take a page from his book."

The last thing she needed was his help. But it would be better than his threats.

Josiah did not like her advice at all. His face turned the colour of beet juice and his fists closed tightly. Aminda quickened her step.

They were almost to the mill. She stepped onto the dam and crossed over. Josiah on her heels.

"Josiah, go home," she said carefully when they reached the other side of the walkway. "Whatever it is you want from me, I don't have it. I am not interested in a match with you. And your threats and attempts at blackmail are not helping."

He snatched at her arms, pulling her roughly to him.

She kicked him in the shin and then stomped on his foot.

The words that came out of his mouth were not meant for mixed company but he gripped tighter, instead of letting go.

"It's not only you I want," he hissed. "Although I could bed you in a second if I chose. Right here. No one around to see or hear."

He was right. The mill was silent, the bridge below was empty, and her father would not wake. Aminda's bravado began to falter.

Josiah was close enough to look down at her breasts. His breath, though foul, had no hint of alcohol this time. He was sober. And dangerous.

Aminda fought his grasp and stomped on his foot again. He grimaced, but kept talking through clenched teeth. "I want the gold. The pirate's treasure. You know where it is. With the miller's daughter, and a chest full of gold..."

"I don't know what you are talking about," Aminda interrupted. But her voice, to her infernal frustration, said otherwise.

His eyebrows lifted, and his grin widened. "Oh, I think you do. And you're going to show me."

"If I did know about any pirate gold, which I don't, you would be the *last* person I would show it to! Now let go of me!"

"Or what?"

Something moved on the other side of the mill. Aminda took a chance.

"Or I'll scream."

"No one will hear. They're all snug in their homes eating cold Sunday roasts." He flicked his wrist and somehow grasped both of her hands in one. How did he *do* that? The other reached around her and grasped at her from behind, forcing her closer.

That was enough. Aminda took a deep breath and let loose the loudest bellow she could. His hand left her behind, slapped across her mouth and then shook her violently, but it was too late. The sound of footsteps echoed across the stream, speeding up and coming their way. Aminda tasted the copper of her own blood.

Josiah heard the footsteps behind him on the walkway and dropped her arms like burning coal.

Aminda rubbed her arms and kicked him in the shin again for good measure.

"You brute!" she yelled, dramatically. "Get your hands off me!" She didn't care who it was, she wanted them to know that this was not of her doing.

The walker was Aunt Mary. Of *all* people! Anyone but Aunt Mary!

Aunt Mary shuffled toward them like an angry goose. She had the nerve to look at Aminda like *she* was at fault. Like Aminda had done something horrible by staving off Josiah's lecherous advances! *Honestly!*

Mary walked up to the two of them, bobbed Josiah a curtsey and shot Aminda a look. Josiah nodded back innocently.

"Aminda Ingerham!" she chastised. "Stop making such dreadful noise. One would think you were a savage! Mr. Cameron is a respectable young man. He doesn't deserve such treatment! I was coming your way to give you these cakes, but with such a display of behaviour I have changed my mind! Josiah, would you take these to your father with my regards?"

Mary handed Josiah the small basket she was carrying. "I'm sorry for my niece's behaviour. She lacks a mother's discipline."

Aminda stood there with her mouth hanging open, unable to believe Aunt Mary's reaction. It wasn't her fault her mother had died! And...and he was assaulting her! In broad daylight! Why was Aunt Mary yelling at her as if she were some common strumpet? Was she blind?

The old hag could shove her cake. She wanted nothing to do with it. It would probably taste like dirt anyway.

With not a word more, Aminda turned and fled to the safety and the sanity of her own home, slamming the door and rattling the bolt across. Cursed or not, at least her father loved her for who she was.

Aminda waited until she was sure Josiah and her aunt

were gone and then opened the door to let the warm spring air into the cabin. She spent the rest of the day setting her house to order. The bread, for once, had risen perfectly and she baked it in the Dutch oven while she set a joint to stew. She churned the cream to butter and set the buttermilk aside for tonight's biscuits.

When the cooking was done, and after a thorough check for Josiah the ingrate, she went outside to the barn. She not only fed Shadow, she also gave him a good grooming. The day was fine, and she considered taking him out for a ride. Perhaps she would go before the sun went down this evening.

She mucked out the barn, then after a quick wash, set to cleaning the cabin from top to bottom. According to Pastor Brown she was already damned. It was probably better to be clean on Sunday and be damned than to live in a hovel. And when in all of her busy life did she have time to keep the cabin clean? Sunday or not, she had work to do.

She scrubbed, swept, washed and shined the place until her fingers were waterlogged and her mind was clearer. Then she sat down to a slice of fresh baked bread and fresh churned butter in the chair beside her father's bed. She sipped tea and grasped her mother's Bible from the shelf.

Aminda knew the Bible. She had learned verses from the time she was old enough to talk. The Bible she knew talked of love and forgiveness, helping and sharing. Somehow the village of Kingsclear had lost that. And she seemed to be bearing the brunt of it.

Would any of this have happened if her mother was still alive? She remembered her mother's kind words and soft hands. She had smelled of strawberry preserves and lye soap. What would her mother think of all of this? She would probably tell Aminda to look around, think a bit, pray even more, and get down to the business of living.

That was exactly what Aminda intended to do.

She looked around.

There was a roof over her head, food in her hand and at least one person who loved her. And maybe another who loved her too.

Now *that* she could think about. Patrick. Her stomach twinged just thinking his name. She wished he had been there today when Josiah had pulled his stunt. What would he have done? Aminda realized that she cared a whole lot more what Patrick thought than what anyone else did. Did that mean she loved him? What exactly did it feel like to love someone? Josiah did not love her in the least. She was a prize, that was all, and a means to get rich quickly.

Patrick had said she was beautiful.

She stood up and walked over to the small looking glass her father used for shaving. Her chestnut hair was long and healthy. Strands escaped from her braids and bun and curled around her face. Her skin was clear and a light dusting of freckles powdered her nose. She was slim, strong and healthy. She supposed she was pretty, but beautiful? Bah. Princesses were beautiful. And she certainly was not one of those.

There were seven more days until the Whitebeard returned. Seven days until her father would be well. Seven more days until the world would be normal. Would there really be treasure? She doubted it. She didn't need gold, she needed her father back. Patrick could have the gold. He needed it more. She'd even hide it for him if he wanted her to, so that his father couldn't find it.

She walked back to her father's side and grasped his arm, moving it back and forth, over and over again. Methodically, she did the same for his leg, and then the same on the other side. It took effort and some grunting, but she managed to roll her father onto his side. Tonight she would turn him to his back. Tomorrow she would roll him onto his other side.

All of the while she prayed for her father, her own safety and that all of this would resolve itself. She prayed for Patrick and his huge family. For the men who had not returned from their outing. And that the tide of belief would not turn against her.

She felt better after that.

And so she got on with the business of living.

Monday, Tuesday and Wednesday were the same except for one thing. Only her cousin Caroline came. Aunt Mary had had enough. Perhaps her prayers had worked.

CHAPTER 7

SAFEGUARDS

CAROLINE WAS AS SWEET AS Aunt Mary was sour. As soon as she got over her fears, she was actually a comfort to have around. She worked away at little tasks around the house and after Aminda showed her how, she actually helped feed her sleeping uncle. She was a whiz at kitchen tasks, and when she realized she could eat whatever she cooked, she began to prepare a treat for the two of them each day. Aminda began to worry she'd develop wide thighs like Mrs. Long with all of the baked goods Caroline concocted.

There was no sign of Josiah, which was a good thing, but also no sign of Patrick, which wasn't.

Aminda was particularly drowsy one evening, sitting by the fire and full of fresh fried sausages, when it happened once again.

She had set a stick on the fire and was watching it to make sure it caught when the vision started. Slowly at first, with the hypnotic swirl of black and yellow holding her eyes against her will. She saw more flames. Her father's mill was engulfed and Patrick and Josiah were inside. They were fighting over something...she could not see what. But in their anger they were ignoring the threat of the flame. She wanted to scream at them both. *Stop it! Look around you!* But they wouldn't hear. She watched in horror as a beam cracked and bent toward them both, and they were lost to the scorching heat.

She came back to reality, struggling for breath. She could feel the heat of the fire on her skin. Her mind whirled. *The mill! In flames! Patrick and Josiah inside!*

No! This was one vision she wouldn't...couldn't let happen. Josiah could burn as far as she cared, but Patrick and the mill could not. It would not come to pass. She wouldn't let it.

Aminda spent the night planning. The mill was made of wood. The tallow that greased the wheels was flammable, as were the logs and gates. The water below kept the ground level damp and safe. She had to protect the upper level. But how? She worried and thought until her eyes closed and she drifted off to sleep.

When Caroline arrived in the morning, Aminda was ready to put her plan into action.

She left early so as to arrive before the men. Nevertheless, Mr. Stairs was sitting on a barrel by the door when she arrived.

"Miss Ingerham," he said, touching his cap.

"Mr. Stairs," she replied and bobbed a quick curtsey. "I'm glad you're here. I need to talk to you before the men arrive."

He raised his eyebrows, but said nothing.

She unlocked the door and walked inside, motioning for Mr. Stairs to follow.

"I had a small blaze in my house last night," she lied, "nothing serious, but it got me to thinking about the mill. This is my father's livelihood, and therefore my own. I've always been wary of fire...and everything in the mill, save a few of the gears, is flammable. It makes me nervous, so I want to protect it. And I want the orders to come from you—the men will be much more likely to listen to you."

Mr. Stairs sat silently.

Aminda plowed on. "I'd like to purchase five rain barrels from the cooper and have them placed on the roof. I'll also have two barrels for this floor and the floor above. with two buckets for each. The roof barrels can collect their own water. The floor barrels we will fill from the stream. If there is any chance of a fire, we can tip the roof barrels over and we can put out any fire on the floors with the buckets before it gets started. The men are not to smoke near the building. I'll bring a sand bucket by tomorrow and they can empty their pipes into it."

That was the best she could do. She waited for Mr. Stairs's response.

He thought for a moment, and then spoke. "Aye, Miss. 'Tis smart to avoid fires, 'specially with the dry season coming on. The men won't be too happy about the smoking bit, but it's true that it would only take a spark. I'll see it's done. The men aren't big on change, but they'll see sense soon enough."

Aminda relaxed a bit. The vision of the flaming beam above the two young men danced behind her eyes. She had to prevent it.

When the men came in, Mr. Stairs picked the least argumentative men and sent them on an errand to the cooper's. Before they left, he told the whole group of the smoking rule. They moaned and groaned. The worst was Mr. Jones. He cursed and spat on the ground.

"Smoke me pipe outside in the rain? Why should I do that?"

"Because if ye don't you'll lose yer dram!" replied Mr. Stairs. "The mill is as dry as a tinderbox and an eejit like you could set it ablaze in an instant. It's smoke outside, or find a new line of employment."

Aminda loved Mr. Stairs. She could never have the courage

to talk to Mr. Jones like that.

Mr. Jones grumbled but didn't leave. He turned and faced Aminda. "This is yer doin', I warrant." The look he gave her was pure ice. Aminda stared back with as much force as she could. She said nothing.

Aminda checked the gears and waited for the pin to be pulled The wheel sprung to life and the whine of the saw filled the air. She nodded to Mr. Stairs and set off toward home.

Mr. Jones was just as confrontational at break. He took his dram with an evil look in his eye. When he turned to go, he spat on the floor beside Aminda's feet, spraying her skirt with dark phlegm. Aminda glared at him, but held her tongue. Mr. Jones was an ass, but she would not rise to his bait.

By quitting time, two barrels had been placed on each floor. They were filled with water from the headpond. Five more sat beside the stairs, waiting to go on the roof. Mr. Stairs assured her that they would be up first thing in the morning, as soon as the dew was dry. Aminda breathed a sigh of relief. The vision haunted her.

Mr. Jones was still belligerent but had lost some of his force. He accepted his dram and his day's wages with no comments. She watched from the door as he lit up his pipe. He blew smoke at her face and walked away.

She checked the gears and the gates with Mr. Stairs, and locked the door. Mr. Stairs seemed anxious.

"Is there something the matter, Mr. Stairs?" she asked.

"No, miss, nothing the matter...I was just wondering how the master is doing. Any change?"

"No...no change, I'm afraid."

"Oh. It's just the men are starting to get antsy. They aren't the most reliable lot. Don't like..." he stopped.

"They don't like taking orders from a woman," Aminda finished. "Well, they'll have to deal with me for a bit longer.

I hope to see some change soon. He's fine though. Just... sleeping. Would you like to come and see for yourself?"

He shook his head violently. Aminda half expected him to make the sign of the devil when she turned her back.

"No! Thank you, Miss. I'll take your word for it. Is there anything you need, though? I know...some of the other villagers...they aren't kind."

Now that was an understatement. No one had been kind. Well, except for Patrick and little Caroline—although she was family, so it didn't really count.

Aminda thought for a few seconds. Mr. Stairs had caught her off guard. She smiled, heartened that not *everyone* in the village thought she was Satan's spawn. The barn chores were getting done, she had enough to eat, and the house was clean.

"That is really very kind of you, Mr. Stairs. Right now I think I'm okay. If you can keep the men working, the mill wheel turning and the gossip to a bare minimum, I would be grateful. When father is well enough to come back, I want the mill to look as it did when he fell sick." There really wasn't anything else he could do. But it was good to have at least one heartfelt offer.

"I'll let you know, though, if anything else comes up."

He gave her a brief nod, turned and headed up the hill toward the village.

Aminda scanned the trees and the road for signs of danger. Josiah, her main source of peril right now, was nowhere to be seen. She walked along the dam, scanning the wheel and the gates. A gentle rain had begun to fall and the wood planks were slippery. All seemed in order. No source of fire. The dampness in the air would protect the roof. And there was lots of water in the headpond if a spark threatened the mill.

Caroline was stirring dumpling dough when Aminda

opened the door to the cabin. The smell of chicken stew masked the smell of the sick room. There was a fresh-baked strawberry pie cooling on the cabinet. How had she done that so fast? It all smelled delicious.

A brief memory lit in her mind of walking into their kitchen in Connecticut. Her mother was working in the kitchen. Betsy, the scullery maid, was helping her cook. Three pies were cooling on the table, and the smell of roast chicken wafted through the air. They were expecting company of some sort. Aminda hadn't cared. All she cared about were the berry pies that were tickling her nostrils. It was sweet torture. And then, from behind her back, her mother had pulled a tiny, flaky, beautiful pie for Aminda alone. It had smelled just like the pie in front of her now.

Caroline smiled at her as she closed her eyes and breathed deeply.

"Carrie, that smells absolutely delicious. Where did you learn to cook so well?"

The praise was well deserved and gratefully received. "Father's sister. She comes twice a week to dine with us. She's a widow in Sainte Anne's but loves to cook. She taught me everything. Mother can feed us, but Aunt Eileen could make a turnip taste like toffee." She giggled. "Mother's cooking makes everything taste like turnips," she whispered.

"It's so much fun cooking for you, because you have everything I need, no one to get in my way, and you appreciate it a lot more than the little piglets at my house." She nodded at Aminda's hat. "Is it raining out?"

"Yes, it just started. The path is a bit slick, though."

Caroline smiled widely. "Mother said if it rained I could stay! That is, if you don't mind... please?"

Aminda grinned back. "Of course you can stay. I would love that. Would you mind sleeping with me upstairs though?"

"Oh, I don't think I'd want to sleep down here. I like Uncle Jonas. Really I do. But I don't think I could sleep down here beside him. And it would be so fun to talk to you up there while we are falling asleep! We can talk about books, and stories, and...all kinds of things!"

"Then it's settled. You'll stay here out of the rain and join me for supper, pie and late night chats."

And that's what they did. The stew and dumplings were hearty and warm in Aminda's stomach, and the strawberry pie was even better with a bit of freshly whipped cream. The girls ate, and talked, all evening. Caroline was such a cheerful guest that the cabin seemed a warm and happy place. Even Mr. Ingerham looked better once they had gotten him to swallow some mashed stew and berries.

Aminda was the most relaxed she had been in weeks. For such a tiny girl, Caroline had an opinion on everything and anything going. It was so refreshing to let herself enjoy the moment instead of wondering what was coming at her next.

Caroline had just started on boys and school and who was more likely to become her beau when there was a knock on the door.

Aminda froze. Who would come calling in this storm?

"Who is it?" She called, trying not to let her wariness leak into her voice.

"Patrick O'Brien."

Her tension evaporated and a broad, silly smile spread across her face. "Oh! Patrick! Just a second!" She wiped her face and hands on her apron, smoothed her hair and unlatched the door. The candles flickered in the damp wind as she did so.

She tried to act natural but had a sudden urge to giggle uncontrollably. Caroline watched her cousin closely, suspicion dawning.

"Please! Come in," she called to her visitor. The temperature in the cabin must have gone up.

It really was Patrick. He was soaked through, but smiling. He wrung his hat out on the veranda and wiped his feet on the brush before coming through the door.

Aminda checked her urge to run to him. She smiled demurely and nodded towards Caroline.

"My cousin, Caroline, and I were just having some fresh-baked strawberry pie. Would you like a slice?"

Patrick's dark hair was plastered to his forehead. His coat was black with rain. He would know Caroline from school, but he acted as if she were a newfound friend.

He bowed gallantly. "Greetings, cousin Caroline," he said. A small puddle of mucky water formed at his feet where he stood. Then he sniffed appreciatively.

"Strawberry pie? What is the occasion? Are we celebrating?"

Caroline blushed at his formal bow. "No occasion. Except for me liking to cook... and being happy that I'm staying with Aminda tonight," she replied shyly.

"Well, lovely young lady, Aminda should be honoured. And yes, I would love a slice of strawberry pie." He winked roguishly at Aminda.

"Patrick, are you cold? Would you like to sit by the fire? Perhaps some tea with your pie?" Aminda asked her questions in rapid succession.

"Yes, yes and yes," he said, chuckling. "The rain is chilly, I am very soggy and would love to sit by the fire to warm my bones and dry my clothes. And hot tea would be just the thing."

He pulled off his wet boots and lifted them over to the hearth. Then he pulled the rocking chair as close as he could to the coals and sat happily.

"What brings you out in such horrible weather?" Aminda

asked. She hoped it was her.

His eyes held hers for a secret moment. Aminda felt the something rise in her belly. "I was in the village conducting some business for my father...and I had to visit the blacksmith for a new hoe blade." He took a quick sip of hot tea and then pulled the blade from a pocket in his coat.

"The blacksmith was none too happy to see me, but a few coins changed his mind. His son was nowhere to be seen," he finished quietly. Aminda was glad of that.

"I suspect Josiah Cameron has a sore foot this week," Aminda said.

"Oh?"

"He...tripped...on his way back from the services." She shuffled her foot out quickly as if she were kicking away a mouse then smiled, rolling her eyes toward Caroline.

"Oooh... He tripped," Patrick said, grinning.

Caroline piped up from behind them. "Josiah Cameron is a mean, nasty brute. He threatened to kill Maisiecat's kittens. I think my ma was sweet on his father when she was younger." The last few words came out in a rush. She went suddenly quiet, her eyes uncertain.

"I don't doubt it," said Patrick. "And he's...clumsy too." He grinned at Aminda. "Did you see him trip?"

"Yes, as a matter of fact I did. I...'ran in to him'...on the way home from services Sunday morning. He was most interested in a rumour he had heard. And in my private life too, I'm afraid. Then, his toe got...stubbed and he hit his leg on something. Limped home just as Aunt Mary came by."

"Oh, I see. And you made it home safely?" he asked, an unspoken question within his question.

"Thankfully, yes. Aunt Mary was not interested in our discussions. She decided to give Josiah her cakes. And Josiah decided to go home." Aminda's eyes flashed. She would have liked to clobber the both of them.

"Oh, *I* baked those cakes for *you*!" Caroline said. "And mother gave them to him? But...why would she do that?"

"I think your mother was under the assumption that I was being rude to Josiah. It was, in fact, the other way around... but she gave him your gift to share with his father, and then he walked her home."

"Well, I never!" Caroline said, hands on hips. "Those cakes were for you!"

"Don't worry, Carrie. I think your mother is angry at me. She wants Josiah to court me and I would rather he not. In fact, I would rather he go soak his head," she grinned. "Besides, you made me the best strawberry pie ever tonight! Oh, and we were going to give some to Patrick."

The girls bustled around, serving pie (they each had another slice) and whipped cream.

Patrick accepted his pie, proclaiming its excellence with every bite. "I have never, ever, tasted such delectable strawberry pie. Such flaky crust. Mmmm. Just the right touch of sweetness. Mmmm. Miss Caroline, you can bake for me any day."

Caroline giggled and blushed.

When they were finished and the dishes cleared, the three of them sat, chatting amiably by the fire. Patrick knew just how to flatter Caroline. Aminda had never seen her so animated. And occasionally, in between jokes and laughter, he would smile at Aminda. Her heart would beat faster at the slightest look.

"And then the silly donkey took off running into the woods, my boot in his mouth and the plow bumping him on the behind all the way!" he finished with a flourish. Caroline was shaking with laughter. Aminda's eyes ran and sides hurt.

"Oh! Patrick, stop!" Caroline screeched. "I've drank too

much tea! Drat. I'll be right back!" And she grabbed her coat and ran out the back door.

Patrick and Aminda were alone by the fire, Aminda's father breathing peacefully on his bed.

"Josiah didn't hurt you, did he?" Patrick asked, all seriousness.

"No, Mary came along before he could do any serious damage. Just a bruise on my wrist." She pulled her sleeve up to show him the fingerprints still visible on her arm. "It's nothing. I'm sure his shins look worse," she said, smiling.

Patrick gently reached out and took her hand in his. He examined the marks, then softly pressed his lips to each one.

Aminda gasped. Her chest had butterfly wings in it.

His lips were soft, but his eyes were dark. "I'm sorry," he said, his voice rough.

"It's not your fault," Aminda said breathlessly.

"Yes, it is. I shouldn'ta left you alone. Josiah Cameron is a dangerous swine. He deserves to be keel-hauled."

"Patrick, you have no choice but to leave me alone. Your family needs you more than I do. I can take care of myself."

His eyes caught hers. His fingertips caressed her cheek, then smoothed back a loose tendril of hair.

"You are brave, like my mother," he said, tenderly. "And strong. It's true, I can't protect you both all of the time. But my father is sober now, and has started to help more..."

"Patrick, I'll be fine. It's only a few more days 'til the Whitebeard comes back. I can last that long. When Father wakes up he will be furious if he hears you have been staying here unchaperoned. Besides, I think Josiah will stay away for a few days. It's not really me he wants. He wants the gold."

"What? He knows about it?"

"Somehow. He knows I have the map."

"That's not good."

"No. And there's another thing, the Pastor at services has begun preaching about curses and evil. He spent the entire sermon looking directly at me. I think the villagers are getting restless. I'm afraid they'll start talking witchcraft. And I'm afraid Josiah will fuel their prejudices if I don't... give in to his advances."

His hand stopped its caressing and grasped her shoulder firmly.

"You are not a witch. I can witness for you."

"But what if they turn against you, too? They don't like different. Especially when it comes to religious beliefs. You don't go to their services. You're suspect without any association with me!"

"We just need to lay low for a while. Wait it out. When your father revives, it will be okay."

"Patrick?" she asked, her hand grasping his for support.

"Yes?"

"Why did you come here tonight? Was it just to check up on me?"

He looked into her eyes. "Partially. I wanted to see you."

Aminda blushed, but did not let go of his hand.

"I'm glad you came," she said.

"But I knew about the villagers talking. So I wanted to give you this."

He searched in his pocket and fished out something. With his other hand he pulled her hand down and opened it, then placed a small object on her palm.

"I made it for you. For protection of a different sort."

It was a small carved wooden cross, covered in intricate Celtic knot work. It had a hole at the top, through which he had threaded a thin leather cord.

"Patrick, it's beautiful."

He took it from her hands and put it around her neck,

tying a knot behind her head. He was incredibly close. His breath tickled. His hands slid down from her neck and rested on her back. He leaned forward, brushing his lips on her forehead, her eyebrows, her cheek...her lips.

Aminda leaned toward him. Her hands knotted themselves in his damp hair. She felt weak and invigorated at the same time. It felt so good to be close to him. So safe.

His lips were soft, tasting of strawberries and cream.

Caroline came crashing through the back door.

They broke apart in an instant, sitting back on their chairs. Aminda smoothed her hair back abstractedly. Patrick cleared his throat.

Caroline's hair was soaked and her eyes were wide.

She giggled.

"It's okay," she said with a devious smile. "I won't tell."

Aminda hadn't realized she'd been holding her breath. She let it out in one big gush.

Patrick stood up, grinning sheepishly. "I should go. My compliments to the cook," he said as he bowed. "That was the most delicious pie."

Caroline continued to smile while she curtseyed.

He turned and faced Aminda. "I'll stay as close as I can," he said. "And I'll try to stop by every day if I can get away." He bowed to her, and Aminda curtseyed back.

"Thank you for your gift," Aminda said as he slipped on his boots and headed towards the door. She grasped it in her hand and smiled. "I will look forward to your visits."

He tipped his hat one last time and walked out into the rain.

"Patrick O'Brien is your beau?" Caroline asked mischievously.

Aminda felt as if she'd had the rug pulled out from under her feet and she'd fallen, hard, on her head. She stood and looked at the door, dazed and glassy eyed. Her hand floated up to her lips.

"Is he?" Caroline asked again.

Aminda swivelled her head to look at Caroline.

"Oh. Um...well, I suppose he is," she said. "I don't generally go around kissing strange young men."

Caroline giggled. "Really? He's very handsome. And he's nice," she said, and shrugged. "Better him than Josiah Cameron. He scares me. Patrick makes me laugh."

Aminda grinned. "He is handsome, isn't he?" And he made her feel weightless. As if all of her world's problems had floated away.

She walked over to the table and poured some water into the basin to wash up. Caroline followed her. Aminda rolled up her sleeves, but before she could plunge her hands into the soapy water Caroline saw the bruises above her wrists. It was blatantly obvious what had caused them.

"Aminda! Who did that to you? It wasn't Patrick was it?" Caroline blurted out.

Aminda tried to cover her wrists with the water. "No! Not Patrick," she said quickly.

"Then who? You can*not* tell me those got there on their own. And don't worry. I won't tell anyone. Just like I won't tell about you kissing Patrick O'Brien."

Aminda believed her, but still, she was reluctant to bring Caroline into this. She was so young...well, not really that young. Caroline was the same age that Aminda was when her mother died and left her to mind her father's house.

"Aminda?"

"You must promise not to tell anyone. Especially your mother."

Caroline drew an X over her heart with her finger. "Cross my heart and hope to die."

"Well, you don't have to go that far. But if you must know, it was Josiah Cameron."

Caroline's young brow crinkled. "That boy is a menace! I heard he was bothering Sissy Perley too. Did he hurt you badly?"

Aminda conceded and pulled her hands from the water, showing the bruises to Caroline. "No. Not really. I kicked him in the shins and stomped on his toes."

"Did you really? Bet that showed him."

Aminda nodded. "As hard as I could."

"Then *that's* why his foot is hurting him."

Aminda wiggled her foot. "These pinchy shoes are good for something, anyway."

Caroline was silent for a minute. "Aminda, can I tell you a secret? And can you promise not to tell anyone?"

Aminda expected Caroline to tell her about her own beau, but instead she heard something different.

"About three weeks ago...just before Uncle Jonas fell ill, and when father was away at Sainte Anne's, I was looking for Maisiecat and her kittens. I went up into the hay loft and heard someone else up there. They were making weird noises. I peeked around the hay to see who it was and saw...and saw Mother. And Josiah's father. They were...laying down. On the hay in the loft. Kissing. I don't think she saw me, but I ran out of the barn as quickly as I could."

Aminda was shocked. So that was why Aunt Mary was so sweet on Josiah Cameron. She was playing the trollop with his father!

Caroline was obviously upset. "That's not all. I ran out to the chicken coop, afraid that they had seen me and would be angry at me. And I ran right into Josiah! He was looking for his father. When he saw me alone he turned all funny. He started talking about how I was becoming a woman. And

I was going to need a beau soon. He tried to...touch me. He said I had to let him or he'd tell everyone I was a...a...a little whore! But I stomped on his foot and ran away into the house as fast as I could!" Her still-girlish hands were clenched by her sides. A tear slid down her cheek.

Aminda wiped her hands and pulled her cousin into her arms. She stroked her hair as a few more tears escaped from Caroline's eyes.

"You did the right thing, Carrie," she soothed. "Josiah should not have done that. And neither should your mother." Aminda could not believe that her uptight aunt could be such a hypocrite. Committing adultery! And with Mr. Cameron! Aminda fumed.

Josiah Cameron had to be stopped. She could understand his lecherous advances towards her. They were the same age. And she was, in the eyes of the village, an eligible young woman. Although it was twisting things to call it courting, he'd only kissed her, albeit violently, but in this society it would be overlooked.

But she would not allow him to attack Caroline. Obviously Mary was too biased and too ignorant to look after her own daughter. Aminda would have to do it for her.

"Carrie, would you like to stay with me for a few days?" Aminda asked. "I could ask your mother. I might be even able to pay you. Just a few shillings a week, but it would be pay. You could be my maid and my cook. But really we'd be friends. I need the help, and we both need to stay away from Josiah Cameron. Patrick promised to come by and check on me, so he'd just have two of us to peek on."

"Oh! Really? Would you do that for me? I could help you keep house while you look after the mill. It would be so much more fun than mother's endless list of chores! Could you really ask her?"

Aminda nodded. "I would love that too. You could walk to school with me when classes are in, and it will just be until father gets better, but I'd love to have some company."

It was settled. Aminda would ask Aunt Mary for permission for Caroline to stay.

The two girls finished their clean up, locked the door and climbed the narrow stairwell to the loft. Caroline was positively vibrating with excitement, her disturbing story forgotten in the thrill of their little scheme.

She eventually ran herself down and fell asleep snuggled into the crook of Aminda's arm. Aminda stroked her young cousin's hair and stared at the boards in the rafters. Her other hand caressed the delicate ridges and knots of the cross which lay on her breast.

Why did things have to be so complicated? Mary's adulterous acts with Mr. Cameron, Josiah's perverse advances toward her cousin and herself, the villagers at the church, the Whitebeard's gold, her vision of the burning mill, Patrick...

Her mind twisted and twirled like the flames in her dream. It was a long time before she fell asleep.

CHAPTER 8

WOOL AND WHISPERS

AUNT MARY WAS AS CONTRARY as the nursery rhyme the next morning in her stuffy kitchen. Aminda was tempted to bring up Mr. Cameron as she stood in front of her, but held her tongue. It would only make things worse, and she had enough problems to deal with right now.

The men had complained under their breaths about women in the mill when she opened the doors that morning. Mr. Stairs had his work cut out for him. The barrels were going up, and the men were not pleased with having to climb to the roof. Mr. Stairs refused to bow to their belly-aching.

So it was out of the frying pan and into the fire...from grumbling men to self-righteous women. Walking Caroline home had been the only high point of her day. She stood in front of her aunt, waiting for an answer.

"I don't rightly know," her aunt was moaning. "Caroline is my main helper in the kitchen." Slave, more like. "Without her Jessica will have more chores. And she's only nine. And sickly..." Jessica was no more sickly than Aminda was. Aminda had watched her whoop the boys in the schoolyard.

She was a strong-willed, sassy lazybones who could do with a little hard work.

"How much did you say you would pay her?" said Mary, searching for the personal benefit. Aminda did not doubt that the girl would be forced to hand over her wages. She would have to give her a separate wage and keep it safe.

"Two shillings a week. Plus room and board."

Mary rocked and considered. Her voluminous stomach shook with the effort. Flies buzzed around the dishes still on the table and the pot hanging over the fire—which was long cold. Aminda waited, cursing the old bat under her breath. For Caroline's sake, Aminda was prepared to beg... but she hoped it wouldn't come to that.

"And she'd get every Sunday evening off, back to work on Monday?"

"Yes. Terms to be renegotiated should father recover." Aminda could just see her Aunt forcing the continued pay, whether Caroline was needed or not.

"Well, I suppose," she finally replied. "You'll be responsible for her, mind you. Should she get into trouble, you will be the one held to account. Not me."

Aminda smiled inwardly. Caroline was the most innocent, well-behaved child in the village. Unlike her harlot of a mother...

"All right, then. I'll agree to it—for now. If I find Jessica's falling short, she'll have to come back, mind you. Can't have my house falling to ruins over a few shillings."

Aminda nodded and held her tongue. Thank goodness. Aminda could not imagine growing up in this environment.

She gritted her teeth and thanked her aunt before escaping out the door.

Aminda had one other errand in the village before she returned to her father. She had been short on sugar and salt after Caroline's baking adventures and needed to replenish her stocks. Perhaps if there was some new cloth at the shop she could pick that up too. She hadn't paid attention until just recently, but her day-to-day dress was threadbare and stained. A new, more flattering neckline couldn't hurt, either...

The plans for her dress consumed her mind as she approached the shop, until the sound of her own name tore her from her reverie.

"Aminda Ingerham barely said a word at the Meeting House on Sunday, not a whisper of the Lord's Prayer. And left before the last notes had been sung!" whined a wheezy voice that could only be Mrs. Long.

"And she was downright rude to Josiah Cameron. Almost pushed him over on her way by," replied Mrs. Grant.

Aminda stopped, curious. She wasn't usually afraid of these old gossip-mongers. But their rumours could grow and spread like wildfires. She stood just outside the door of the shop, the sun beating down on her demurely bonneted head.

"Have you seen Mr. Ingerham since he fell ill? Josiah said he's barely alive. Like the Angel of Death is awaitin' him. Josiah says the very air feels evil in that cabin, and the physician couldn't touch whatever foulness he's come upon. He fears somethin' awful for Miss Aminda. Afraid she's doin' the Devil's work." Mrs. Long's wheeze grew hushed. "And I heard from Mr. Jones that there were dead fish in the headpond last week! Not a mark on 'em. Like they'd been cursed!"

"No!" Mrs. Grant said, her tone eager.

"Yes! And even the gears in the mill are workin' wrong. John Smith cut his hand something terrible at the mill last week..."

He did not! John Smith had cut his hand fishing a week ago. Likely a result of too much rum. Aminda had had enough.

She fixed a very artificial smile on her face and marched through the door.

Mrs. Grant at least had the decency to look embarrassed. She fussed over the simples on the counter and brushed away non-existent dust. "Oh, Miss Ingerham!" she squeaked like a cornered hen. "What a pleasure to see you!"

Mrs. Long merely huffed and stepped back, as if Aminda were a bad smell.

"Thank you, Mrs. Grant. The pleasure is all mine. Truly," she said kindly, but her eyes were ice. She refused to acknowledge Mrs. Long with more than a nod. How dare they speak of her so! And how dare Josiah Cameron suggest she were a devil worshipper! She would do more than kick his shin the next time she saw him.

She ordered her salt and sugar and placed them in her basket. Mrs. Long continued to watch from the side of the counter. A flush crept up Aminda's neck, a mixture of nerves and anger. The air was tense, and Mrs. Grant rushed through the order as quick as her pudgy little fingers would allow.

"Ladies," Aminda nodded, although she thought neither woman deserved the title after listening to their gossip.

"Have a pleasant day!" Mrs. Grant's shrill voice called, but only after Aminda was out of the door and on the road. Pleasant? Unlikely. Not now anyway.

Aminda shook her head and walked down the road, her thoughts crashing around in her skull. Things were more serious than she'd imagined. She knew she was walking a fine line, but hearing things voiced so openly had rankled her. Blast Josiah Cameron for spreading such vindictive rumours! And her father too. What was her father thinking, getting her in such an unbelievable mess? Her eyes burned with the injustice of it all. And then, to her infernal frustration, tears began to fall.

106

She stormed up the path and into her cabin, wondering what other annoyances the day would present. Much to her surprise, woodsmoke drifted from the chimney and the door was propped open.

What now?

Aminda stomped up the door ready to blast today's intruder with a piece of her mind...and stopped at the sight of her young cousin's smiling face.

"Aminda! She let me stay!" Caroline squealed, and threw her arms around Aminda's waist. "I ran right back!" she said. Aminda rolled her eyes to the heavens and thanked God that, for once, she had held her tongue.

Caroline was over the moon with excitement. The cabin smelled warm and spicy from baking ginger snaps, a nice counterpoint to Mary's chilly reception and the villagers' accusatory one.

They had their treats and headed out to the barn to do the chores. The sheep desperately needed to be relieved of their winter coats, so the girls spent the rest of the morning fighting with disgruntled half-naked ewes. Both of them had helped parents with the chore, but neither of them had done it on their own. They chased the crabby sheep and held onto them by their legs, heads and whatever else they could grab while Aminda sheared. At one point, a particularly contrary ewe stuck her hoof up Aminda's nose. And shortly afterwards another head-butted her backwards into the manure pile.

Caroline tried not to laugh, really she did, but the sight of her sedate cousin, hair sticking up every which way, fleece covered, spattered with mud and sitting awkwardly in sheep poo was too much. She dissolved into giggles. Fleece erupted out of her nose like smoke. And then Aminda started. The two of them abandoned all sense of propriety and laughed and laughed and laughed.

By the time they were done, they were filthy, fleecy and completely exhausted. Caroline set about making a fire to boil and clean the fleeces in while Aminda made an attempt at ordering her hair and clothing. She headed down to the mill and the afternoon dram rations with a light heart.

By sundown, the girls had washed and picked most of the fleeces. Aminda was in the loft searching for the carding blocks when Patrick knocked on the door.

She rushed down the stairs, forgetting what a state her clothes were in.

Patrick took one look and smiled, turning to Caroline.

"I see you and your cousin have been...fighting with the sheep," he said to her.

Caroline giggled. "You can say that again. Ask Aminda about the manure pile," she said, a grin on her face.

He swivelled to face her, eyes questioning, the corners of his mouth twitching.

Aminda flopped down in a chair by the table. "Go ahead. Laugh away," she said. "I swear that ewe was possessed."

Patrick's mouth was in a full smile.

"Well, she was," Aminda pouted. "Seriously!"

Caroline nearly collapsed with the effort not to laugh while Aminda blew at the hair dangling in her face. A fluff of fleece flew into the air and promptly landed on Aminda's nose. Her eyes crossed to watch it. Caroline exploded into laughter closely followed by Patrick. It was infective. Aminda chuckled, then giggled and then held her side with uncontrolled mirth.

How good it was to laugh! Aminda's eyes watered and her sides hurt, but she let it come. It felt so good to sit with friends and be herself. When the impromptu laugh-fest slowed down, Patrick came and sat at the table, joining them for some ginger snaps and tea. He was happy to hear that Caroline was more or less permanently staying with Aminda.

He also glanced meaningfully at Aminda when the Sunday night off was mentioned. Caroline would be safely ensconced at her home, slaving away for her lazy mother, while they were digging for cursed treasure. It was a perfect solution all around.

He stayed just long enough to finish his tea, then headed home before the sun set and he was missed.

Aminda felt torn when he left, even knowing that she would see him again in a day or two. It felt as if a part of her walked out the door with him. She shook her head at herself. She was turning into a silly-headed floozy! He was just a boy. A nice boy, a handsome boy, but she had no time for boys.

The girls carded wool and chatted by candlelight then fell into their beds with just enough energy to blow out the taper before falling into a white and fleece-filled sleep.

⌒⌒◦⦿◦⌒⌒

Sunday morning came with no sign from Patrick, Josiah or the Whitebeard. Aminda and Caroline locked the door, leaving Turtle on guard, and headed to services, Caroline packed for an overnight at her home with her own wages in her pocket and her mother's wages in her bag. They walked silently, lost in their own thoughts.

Aminda was on edge, wondering what was to come that evening. She was so preoccupied that she didn't even notice Patrick standing in the small stand of trees by the little church.

"Patrick!" Caroline squealed. "Are you coming to services with us today?"

Patrick had been whittling a small piece of wood. He stood up, tipped his hat at Aminda and then turned to Caroline. "No, young miss. My grandfather would turn over in his grave if he heard that I had gone t' the Church of England for services.

109

No, I'll just be waiting here for Miss Ingerham. I heard she had a small bit o' trouble last week, and I'm here to ensure it doesn't happen again." He nodded to the church. Josiah was watching from the door, his eyes far from charitable. Aminda felt a chill go up her spine.

Patrick saluted Josiah with the knife. Josiah turned and headed into the church.

Patrick glanced at Aminda's neck, where his small Celtic cross hung over her Sunday-best dress. He smiled broadly. "I will be waiting here, carving. I'll walk you both home if you'd like."

Caroline giggled. "I would like, but mother will be inside. I'll have to walk home with her. I'm sure Aminda would like you to..." she giggled again.

Aminda would certainly like him to, she thought, for many reasons. The most important of which was self preservation. Josiah was bent on his goal, with increasing forcefulness. Aminda had successfully fought him off a couple of times...she didn't know if she'd be quite so successful the next. Although her virtue was not something she guarded with great care, her health and her life were. Josiah Cameron was dangerous.

Aminda smiled at Patrick. "That would be very kind of you, Mr. O'Brien," she said. "I accept your offer."

The bell clanged for services to begin.

Aminda sighed. This was not going to be fun. "We should hurry in, I'll see you afterwards?" At least there was something to look forward to.

"You will," Patrick replied. "I'll be waiting right here."

Aminda felt somewhat safer. She rushed into the meeting hall after Caroline. Caroline slid in beside her siblings in their family pew. Josiah was in the back. There was a seat at the very front, right in front of the pulpit, and a seat beside Josiah. Aminda chose the hellfire in the front rather than the hellchild in the back. She could almost feel the righteous glares of the parishioners on her back as she sat down.

It was a long sermon. At one point, Aminda actually had to resist the urge to wipe the pastor's spittle off of her face. He was screaming down at her, words of hate and horror as if the fate of the entire world rested on her shoulders.

"...the Evil One has wormed his way into our midst. This *very minute* he is poisoning our village! Infecting innocent souls! We must fight back! God's army needs willing soldiers!" He screamed, red-faced and sweat-soaked.

Really? If this was the Church of England's idea of God, Aminda might have to consider conversion to Catholicism. It would be a lot less damp. And on Saturday night she could just ask for forgiveness. A few Hail Marys and she would be set for the week.

She sat there, ignoring the pastor's ranting and considering her sins. The visions she didn't count as sinful. She didn't ask for them, they just came. In fact, she did everything she could to avoid them. Maybe that was a sin. If they came from God, maybe she should let them come and accept them as prophetic, not fight against their every nuance. The Bible told of several women who were known prophets.

She didn't steal, she rarely lied, she didn't take the Lord's name in vain, and she wasn't married, so adultery was out too.

She had remained chaste all of her life, not really for a sense of duty to God and moral obligation but because she had never met someone she would consider a relationship with, on any level. Josiah made her physically sick. Not to mention a bit frightened. But Patrick...Patrick she wasn't sure about. The feeling in her stomach was awfully strong. She wasn't sure she could fight against it when the time came. The temptation was there, and there was no one to stop her from doing what she liked. But still, she had done nothing to be ashamed of. She had walked a thin line, but her conscience was clear...which was more than she could say about a few of the members of this congregation. Some of the most self-righteous had the most to be ashamed of. She glanced back at Caroline, sitting beside Aunt Mary. Mary's hands were folded in supplication. Her eyes were glued to the pastor. She saw Aminda turn, and glared at her as if she were a naughty toddler.

"...And *witches*! Oh yes! Witches right here on the River Saint John! Wanton women ready to steal your soul!"

Aminda turned back and attempted to sit demurely, avoiding the flying words and spit, waiting for this version of purgatory to end. Her reward for merely enduring awaited her outside. The thought bolstered her spirits.

At last the pastor had sermoned himself hoarse. His moment of drama had passed, and he finished with a closing prayer. Communion was passed. Aminda looked the pastor in the eye without remorse as she said "Amen."

Finally the last strains of the recessional droning from the revived parishioners ended. This time Aminda did not rush. She knew that Patrick was outside. She knew that Josiah wouldn't dare try anything in broad daylight with others around.

She shook the pastor's sweaty hand and carefully descended the steps to the walk. Patrick was still whittling, acting as if he had all the time in the world and all of the right in heaven to be there. Josiah's face was dark, his posture tense. His eyes shot from Aminda to Patrick and then back again. An ugly sneer spread across his uneven features. After a few seconds he appeared to change his mind. He shrugged and stalked off toward his own home, which just happened to be the same way that Mary and Caroline lived.

Aminda felt a twinge of unease as she watched him go

but she shook it off. Surely her young cousin would be safe at home. Aminda's uncle would rest at home all day and Caroline could stick close to him. Mary would not dare meet with Mr. Cameron while her husband was in the house.

Aminda pretended to nod and walk by Patrick. He stood and walked the same way, as if he were merely strolling home. By the time they reached the bend in the road, they were walking side by side. No one else was around.

"Miss Ingerham? Might I join you?" Patrick asked politely.

"Why certainly, Mr. O'Brien," she replied. "Are you going my way?"

"As a matter of fact, I am."

"Would you...care to come for tea, Mr. O'Brien? Or a little refreshment on your journey?" She grinned, following along.

"That would be most pleasant."

They walked along silently for a few steps, until they were absolutely certain they were alone.

"Thank you for walking me home, Patrick," Aminda said, her voice hushed. "Josiah had violence on his mind, and you deterred him. I only hope he doesn't turn his anger toward Caroline."

"Caroline?" he asked. "But she's only a child."

"She told me he had tried before. While Mary was playing the strumpet with his father, no less! Caroline discovered them in the hayloft and then in her distress ran towards the fields...and right into Josiah."

"Was she...hurt?" Patrick's voice spoke quiet fury. He had younger sisters, near the age of Caroline.

"No, she got away from him. She was very shaken. I believe I'm the first one she's told. She certainly couldn't tell her mother."

"That scum. That filthy bastard!" He clenched his fists.

"Patrick, you mustn't tell anyone! Caroline told me in

113

confidence!"

"Oh, I wouldn't tell a soul. But I might beat one to a pulp—not that that eejit has a soul—and leave him to lie in pig shite. He'd feel at home there."

"Well, as much as I'd like to see that, you'll have to wait. Caroline'll be fine tonight. Her father is home, so Mary wouldn't dare have a late night tryst with her lover, and Josiah will hopefully stay away."

"I will deal with him later," he said, and the matter was closed. For the moment.

"Have you heard from the Whitebeard?" Aminda asked.

"Nothing. Mind you, I've been busy." He grinned impishly. "Minding the fields, the little ones, father and you is fairly overwhelming employment."

"But you needn't 'mind' me. I'm fine."

"It's not you I'm worried about so much as those around you. Mill workers, blacksmith's sons, parishioners—even the pastor himself seems against you. What did you do to him to get him so riled up? Holy Mary, I could hear him caterwauling at you all the way across the road!"

Aminda smiled. "There wasn't a single seat in the hall, 'cept one. It was directly in front of him. I'm still damp from the flying spittle," she said dramatically wiping her face with her arm.

"Not much wonder. For someone so sweet, pretty and unassuming, there are a lot who seem bent on damning you."

Aminda blushed, hearing the compliment buried in his words.

Patrick saw her blush and stopped. They were passing through a thicket of trees just before the road rounded a turn and headed down toward the river below. The sunlight filtered through the leaves, dappling the ground with flickering light. He reached out to grasp her hand and pulled her off of the road to a small path she hadn't seen before. It was barely a deer track. He gently pulled her behind him, following the track further into the trees and along the edge of the hill to a clearing the size of a room. She could see the river but not the road or mill. It was silent, secluded and beautiful.

"Oh," she said, surprised by its beauty.

"I found this spot last year...followed a doe to it. She was feeding her fawn, just over there." He pointed to a pine branch. A small soft bed was overhung by its thick coverage.

"It's lovely."

"Here. Sit."

He spread his coat over the needles. They sat. The river sparkled in the late spring sunshine. Purple violets blossomed everywhere and tiny wild strawberries grew all around them.

Aminda picked one and popped it in her mouth. It was sweet, a tiny burst of flavour on her tongue. She picked a few more and offered one to Patrick.

He looked at her silently, bent down and kissed her fingers, slowly. One by one. Aminda shivered.

He took the strawberry gently with his lips, then kissed the stain on her palm.

It was very warm here, in the sheltered sun.

"You are, you know," he said, gazing at her. His finger traced the outline of her chin.

Aminda didn't understand his statement. Not that she was understanding anything well with Patrick so close. A blue jay called in the trees behind them. Aminda jumped.

Patrick reached up and touched her brow, then undid the string of her bonnet. It fell to the ground behind her.

"You're sweet. And more than pretty...you're beautiful. It's torture for me. Just sitting here so close to you." He tucked a stray hair behind her ear—delicately, as if it was spun gold. How could work-calloused hands be so gentle?

"You're not alone," was all Aminda could articulate. She vaguely remembered thinking about this very feeling during the service...

"Alone in what?" he asked, as he carefully removed the clasp from her hair. It tumbled down around her shoulders, a shining chestnut veil.

"The torture part. I'm...having trouble focusing right now."

"Really?" he said mischievously. "What does it feel like when I do this?" He bent forward and kissed her neck softly, just behind her ear.

Aminda caught her breath.

"Like lightning," she gasped.

"And this?"

His fingertip traced her lip, barely touching.

"Like springtime..."

He smiled.

Aminda closed her eyes, sensation overwhelming her. The something in her stomach was wide awake now. And hungry.

"Patrick..." was all she could say.

He stopped.

Aminda opened her eyes. His face was directly in front of hers. His sparkling eyes spoke of yearning. His rough hands were velvet-soft on her cheek.

"Aminda," his voice was deep, husky.

She lay back, his hand held in hers and the forest singing around them.

And when he kissed her again he didn't block out the sun. He let it in.

CHAPTER 9

PREPARATIONS

THEY MADE IT BACK TO the cabin without anyone the wiser. Patrick had told his family that he was going in to Sainte Anne's to search for a new plough blade. He would camp in the woods outside of town and return after he'd visited the shops. He did this often, so they wouldn't expect him until late Monday, if then.

The cabin was quiet when they arrived except for the welcoming whinny of Shadow in the paddock. There was no sign of Josiah. Patrick followed her up onto the veranda and blew on the heat-dampened curls escaping from her hastily re-done bun as she unlocked the door. Her fingers fumbled and she dropped the keys. As she reached down to pick them up, the door opened on its own.

Aminda froze. The door had been locked. She had checked it.

She stood up slowly, alert.

Patrick slid around her, grabbed a stick of wood from the pile beside the door, and gently stepped in front of her. When he was sure she was behind him, he reached out with his left hand and opened the door the rest of the way. He stepped in to the gloom of the cabin.

Someone chuckled.

"Very valiant, young Mr. O'Brien, but unnecessary," a voice said. "I am not here to ravage Miss Ingerham, beautiful though she may be. I believe you were expecting me?"

Finn McKeen sat at the table. A ring of pipe smoke surrounded his head. The light shining through the chinks in the dark cabin made him look ethereal. Ghostlike.

Aminda felt a chill go up her spine. Very different from the one that she had gotten just moments ago.

"I see things have progressed here. Not unexpectedly." His eyes lingered on Patrick's hand, which rested protectively on Aminda's waist.

"Perhaps," Patrick replied.

Finn chuckled again. "You don't have to hide anything from me, boy. I will not condemn you as others would. I have no wish to crush others in the name of religion."

Patrick's hand stayed.

"How did you get in here?" Aminda asked. "The doors were locked."

The Whitebeard snorted and flicked his hand. "Psssht. Simple locks. Not even necessary to use magic against them."

They stood just inside the door, not sure what to do.

"Well, don't just stand there, young lovebirds. I don't usually bite, and as a matter of fact, I have employed my powers of culinary prowess and have prepared you a small meal."

Aminda noticed, for the first time, that the table was set and the kettle was steaming by the fire.

"Coffee, ham and some lovely cheese I picked up in the markets of Sainte Anne's... And I took the liberty of baking some bread, as well. It was quite dull sitting here watching Mr. Ingerham breathe. I needed something to do."

"Well, come on...don't let it get cold." He pointed at the settings. "I'll even let you sit beside each other, so as to not disturb this lovely aura the two of you are projecting..."

Aminda was pretty sure the man was off of his rocker and she wasn't inclined to trust his food—he had cursed her father, after all—but it did smell particularly delicious. Her stomach growled. She hadn't eaten since early that morning and it was now well into the afternoon.

Patrick moved forward, choosing the seat closest to the Whitebeard. He sat down. Aminda followed, sitting on the other side of Patrick. Her thigh pressed against his. The touch made her feel a bit light-headed. The Whitebeard smiled knowingly.

They ate, silently for the most part. The food was as delicious as it smelled, and Aminda and Patrick were both famished. Aminda glanced at him occasionally. The way his dark eyelashes curled upward. The way he held his knife, twirling it slowly while he ate. The way his shoulders curved. It was very distracting.

When she looked away she saw the Whitebeard was staring at her as if she was a specimen on a card. It made her uncomfortable. She focused on her plate, cheeks flushed.

She finished her plate quickly, got up and began clearing the table, offering Patrick more ham.

"Excellent repast, if I do say so myself," said the Whitebeard as he took another slice from the platter she was offering Patrick. "And most interesting company. It's been many, many moons since I've been young and in love. Refreshing to see. I daresay there is much controversy in such a pairing, but I've seen worse."

Was he intentionally embarrassing her? He made it sound like they were a pair of breeding horses. And how dare he comment on their relationship, however it stood! He didn't even know them! The dishes clanked dangerously in the water as she scrubbed them, Aminda barely noticing the clamour. Patrick sat and glared at the Whitebeard across the table. The man was smoking again, filling the cabin with a choking haze. Aminda pointedly stomped over and opened the door to let in fresh air. Finn McKeen puffed away, oblivious to her censure.

When the dishes were finally cleaned, Aminda had chores to do in the barn. She donned the carved clogs she wore for barn work, threw her bonnet over her still-messy hair and headed towards the door.

"Can I help you with the chores?" Patrick asked. He jumped up and followed her without waiting for her answer. Anything to escape the Whitebeard's bizarre manner and scrutinizing gaze.

With two people, the chores took much less time. Patrick gallantly did the heavier work and Aminda fed the chickens, collected the eggs and fed the pigs.

"That man has a lot of nerve," Patrick said quietly as he leaned over the door of the stall Aminda was cleaning out. "Curses your father, practically blackmails us into helping him, breaks into your home, and then has the nerve to treat us like common breeding stock!"

"I know! Honestly. It was driving me insane listening to him go on about us like he was some sort of social commentator in the Times. How dare he? At least the dinner was good." She leaned on her pitchfork as she spoke.

Patrick picked a stray piece of hay out of Aminda's hair. The sun was setting outside, and the glow through the stable door shined orange in the chestnut strands.

"Are you frightened? About tonight that is...?" he asked.

"Frightened? No, not really. I think I'll be relieved when it's all over and father is well again. Although I won't be as free to do things like this..." She leaned over and kissed Patrick's sun bronzed cheek. He closed his eyes, savouring her touch.

"That will be a true shame," he said. "I can't always be off away from the farm either. If Ma and the wee ones are going to eat, I'm going to be the one to provide for them. Unless father continues to stay away from the drink and starts to take responsibility for his household. Maybe there's a spell in McKeen's book for that."

"Patrick, how many brothers and sisters do you have?" Aminda only saw the ones that came to school with him.

"Well, there's Maire, Siobhan, Martha, Claire, Shane and wee Kathleen. And another due in the fall. So if that turns out well, there will be eight. Shane is seven, and will be old enough to help with the ploughing soon. But he's the only other boy."

"Eight children. Wow."

Eight hungry mouths to feed. Eight times enduring what had killed her mother. Aminda had to admit, the way things had been going she was, for the first time in her life, considering what it would be like to be married. She was of age, nearly sixteen, and was healthy. She supposed she would have to marry and have children sooner or later. Father wouldn't leave her the mill unless there was a husband to 'look after things', even if that meant staying out of her way.

Patrick was handsome, no denying that. The setting sun shone in his hair, making him look more like a Greek god than a Catholic farm boy. And of all the boys in the village, he was by far the most reasonable, responsible and reliable. But would her father see that? Would he see the ostracized Irish family? Or would he see the potential son-in-law and companion that could help him as he grows old? Aminda had no idea. Perhaps after tonight she would find out.

Patrick shrugged. "Eight mouths to feed, but also eight

sets of hands to help. On the whole, the girls are great helpers for Ma. They help outside when they can. If I couldn't do the outside work they would still get by." It was as if he had heard her thoughts.

The setting sun turned from orange to red.

"We should get back inside. The barn will do until tomorrow," Aminda said.

"Aye, it will. Wonder what the Whitebeard has in mind."

"We'll soon find out."

He reached out and grasped her hand. "If it gets too dangerous, we must leave. I don't trust the Whitebeard. Your father wouldn't want you to die for him, Aminda. You know that, don't you?"

Aminda nodded, feeling tears spring to the surface. She'd tried to avoid thinking about what tonight meant. If she did not succeed, her father wouldn't wake. If he didn't wake up, he would likely die. She would lose her father, and she would lose the mill—and then what would she do? She would be alone.

She must not fail, for both of their sakes.

CHAPTER 10

TREASURE

THEY WALKED ACROSS THE YARD and up into the cabin. The Whitebeard had changed from his bizarre cloak into a simple shirt and trousers. They were both black. He had braided and knotted his beard. A black cap sat on the table as did two piles of black clothing.

"I took the liberty of purchasing some appropriate garments for tonight. I cannot vouch for the fit, but you need something dark. It would not do for us to be seen.

"Now. Why don't you go and change, then I will tell you a few things that you need to know. Tonight's journey, although interesting, will not be a walk in the park. There are certain conditions, certain rules that I have placed on the treasure which we must all know...but first, go and change." He gestured at the first pile, and then at the stairs.

Aminda figured out that the first pile was for her. She glanced at Patrick, grabbed the pile and climbed the stairs to the loft. She dumped it on her bed, finding a black shirt, lightweight black coat, a black cap and black...trousers. Trousers! She had never worn trousers in her life! Mind you, she hated skirts. But she was not a man. She looked at the pile again, trying to see if anything else was hidden in the folds of the other pieces, but no. Only the four pieces. Nothing else.

Well, if she was going to dress like a boy, she might as well look the part. She slipped on the trousers and the shirt, making sure all of the buttons and ties were done up properly. The trousers rubbed at her legs. She wished she had a proper looking glass so she could see the result and she hoped she didn't look as foolish as she felt. She braided her hair tightly and tied it up in a knot, high on the top of her head. Then she popped the hat over top of it. She rifled through her skirt pocket, found the map and Patrick's hunting knife. Her cross she tucked under her shirt. It couldn't hurt to have it with her.

"Are you finished changing, Patrick?" she called down, knowing Patrick was doing the same thing below.

"Yes, black as night down here!" Patrick called up.

She stepped slowly down the stairs, feeling naked. Without the swish of skirts, and the curves of her body showing clearly, she felt exposed.

"Ah, Miss Ingerham," said Finn. "I trust the sizing is to your liking. I hope you don't mind, but I took the liberty of acquiring trousers instead of skirts for you. Much more practical for night-time excursions into the wilderness."

Aminda had to agree he had a point. Patrick was staring at her with a mixed look of appreciation and dismay. She smiled at him and did a little curtsey. "What do you think?" she asked with a touch of mischief.

"I think it's a good thing Mr. Ingerham is asleep or he'd be after you with a whip. Or after me with a whip for looking at you dressed like that..." he said. His eyes lingered on her legs a little longer than would have been appropriate were they in public.

Finn cleared his throat. "Practicality not seductiveness was the purpose here. Now, you'll have plenty of time to ogle each other in the moonlight. Shall we sit? And discuss our plan?"

Aminda squashed the urge to giggle. She sat, as modestly as a female could sit in men's trousers.

"So. The treasure is hidden well, and one may only find it by following by certain rules. I like rules, and as such bound the treasure from even myself in this way. My mind is a trifle foggy on a few of the details—it has been awhile—but I will tell you what I know.

"Firstly, the treasure may only be found on either the night of the full moon or the night of the new moon. The signs of the treasure's hiding place are only visible on these nights. And the treasure can only be found in the four hours after midnight. We will have to act quickly.

"Secondly, the party searching for the treasure must add up to an odd number. One, three, five...any odd number, but it is difficult to do the work required alone, so three would be the next best number. Hence why your presence and knowledge are fortuitous, Mr. O'Brien.

"Thirdly—and this, I believe, is where your father's party went wrong, Aminda—the treasure search and recovery must take place in complete and utter silence. From the moment we step into our boat, until the moment we return to the dock from whence we started, we must not speak. Not even a whisper. I believe that your father and his party successfully reached their destination and found the hiding place. Unfortunately, they were not aware of this restriction. Or did not observe it. I believe someone spoke and set off the curse. Those who were with the treasure must have perished. Your father made it back with his life—it is likely that he never laid eyes on the treasure. But he was still affected.

"Because we cannot speak, we must devise hand signals, or other ways to communicate. When someone touches their leg, like so," he made to give his leg a large smack, but stopped just before it cracked a sound, "like the beaver almost slapping its tail, it's a warning, be aware. Pointing with one's thumb to one's back means to clear out. Get away as quickly as possible. This will mean go forward, follow." He waggled his fore-finger.

"When I do this," he crossed his arms in an X, "it means slow down or stop. This," he pointed to both eyes with two fingers, "means be wary, watch, see what I do."

Aminda felt like she was back in school having a lesson. Only this time she was sitting with the boys.

"The treasure is hidden not far from the X on the map that Aminda holds. If you get me to the right stream, I should be able to find it from there. I did not write the real whereabouts on the map, only the approximate location. If your father's acquaintances made it to the treasure, they were very observant indeed.

"Patrick, I believe you know where the stream on the map is?"

Patrick nodded. "Two upriver from the mill stream."

"How long do you think it would take to row from here to that stream?"

"Two, maybe three hours. It's not far, and if the wind is low it should be an easy row," Patrick answered.

Finn pulled an intricate watch out of his pocket. He checked it, fiddling with a dial as he did so. "Then we should leave in less than an hour. We will need shovels and axes, which I have bundled outside, and my boat is moored just below the mill."

Aminda spent the last half hour before they left feeding and getting her father settled. His colour was good, but there were some disturbing red marks on his heels. She hoped tonight would be the last night he would lay in his bed motionless.

Even with constant care, this could not go on forever. He could get an infection. Would his sleeping body fight off simple diseases? Or would they fester in his weakened system?

They had to succeed and the Whitebeard's cure had to work.

They left when it was full dark and the moon had just begun to rise. Before they did, Patrick pulled Aminda aside, out of Finn's hearing.

"If something goes wrong, Aminda, get back to the boat. Get away, fast. I still don't trust him. The whole thing makes me nervous. The other men that went with your father never came back. Do you have the knife I gave you?"

Aminda nodded and pulled it from her pocket. She slid it from its sheath and showed it to him. It glinted in the moonlight.

"Good. If you need to, use it."

Aminda nodded again but she wasn't sure she could. She quickly stowed it away.

"If I don't get to tell you again, I want to you to know," he reached down and tilted her chin to him, capturing her eyes with his own. "This past week, though insane, has been the best week o' my life. When all o' this is done, when your father wakes up and the Whitebeard takes his book and vanishes from our lives...I hope to get the chance to court you properly. As a gentleman. With your father's permission."

He bent over and brushed his lips over hers. His finger caressed her temple.

Finn McKeen cleared his throat behind them.

"That's all very touching... but the time has come," was all he said.

They took only one small lantern and kept that shuttered. There was nothing to say, so they remained silent. There was no wind and they saw and heard no one.

The mill loomed large and dark over them as they passed, their footsteps echoing on the wooden boards of the dam. The moon lit their way, casting long shadows into the headpond. Aminda stuck close to Patrick. Their shadows morphed into one as they walked.

Finn directed them along a path to where he had left the boat. Aminda was thankful for the trousers. Skirts would have caught and tripped her up in the grabbing pine boughs. The shadows rippled on Finn's coat.

It was eerily silent in the woods. As they approached the simple boat, Aminda's over-alert ears caught the slap of water against the shore. A bird rustled in the branches above them. The scrape of the boat on the rocky shore seemed too loud in their enforced silence, announcing their position like musket fire. They scanned the river, searching for stray boats and wondering what the night would bring.

As the odd threesome slid into the moonlit night, eyes pointed toward the river, they didn't see a figure dart from behind the mill toward the village. The slap of the water and the burble of the oars hid the rush of tree branches as Josiah Cameron slipped deeper into the shadows.

Finn sat at the front of the boat watching for rocks and logs, his mind occupied by the task ahead. He held the map in his hand. Aminda sat cross-legged on the floor, and Patrick rowed. Aminda was nervous and jumpy, but the gentle *splash-drip* of the oars and the slow, rocking movement of the boat were soporific. She concentrated on the shore, watching for movement. In her head she repeated the same phrase over and over again. *I must not speak. I must not speak. I must not speak.*

It wasn't easy.

There were still so many things that she wanted to say to Patrick. So many questions she wanted to ask Finn. Spending this entire trip in silence seemed like an impossible task. She wished she had brought a handkerchief to tie around her mouth and remind herself to keep quiet.

They stuck close to the shore, watching the rocks and the trees, passing the first stream and continuing on in search of the second.

Splash, drip. Splash, drip. Splash, drip.

More rocks, more trees, more stars and bright moon.

Splash, drip. Splash, drip.

The shore fell away into a deep bay and Patrick angled the boat toward it, hugging the western shoreline.

Finn unshuttered the lantern just enough to see the map. Patrick continued to row.

Splash, drip. Splash, drip.

An owl called and jumped from his branch, swooping low over the boat and frightening Aminda. She jumped, slapping her hand over her mouth to prevent herself from crying out. Her heart pounded in her chest. The bird landed on a tree branch, the soft *whoosh* of his wings audible in the moonlit silence.

The owl watched them from the other shore, his eyes glowing. They slid by, leaving only a brief ripple in the stream.

Splash, drip.

Patrick rowed on, beads of sweat sparkling on his forehead.

After an eternity of still, flat river, the water rippled with current. First gently, then stronger and stronger. Patrick's strokes were tougher and his breath came and went in deep, heavy gasps. The rush of a waterfall appeared ahead. The Whitebeard motioned toward the shore. He pointed to a small, pebbly beach. Patrick pulled the oars and steered the boat to the water's edge. Aminda sat still as the Whitebeard hopped out and pulled them further up. When they were solidly on the beach, Patrick shouldered the bundle of tools and Finn took the lantern and the map. There was nothing left for Aminda to take, so she simply followed along.

They walked toward the waterfall, the murmur of the falls growing into a full fledged roar as they approached. The beach grew slippery and Aminda had to concentrate to keep herself upright and stay silent. The pebbles became rocks and the rocks, boulders. They clambered and climbed until they reached the base of the falls.

Water sprayed and crashed beside them. A large pool swirled just to their left. It sparkled in the moonlight. Aminda could see no bottom.

Above them rose what looked to be a solid rock wall with a few outcroppings. Water cascaded over it, making a shimmering sheet of black glass. It towered over them, at least thirty feet tall. Even if they wanted to speak to one another, no one would hear. The noise crashed in their ears and the ground shook from the water's force.

To their right were more boulders, hung with moss and deadfall. There was no way around the cliff face and the rock face was too steep and too wet to ascend.

Aminda watched in disbelief as Finn McKeen began to climb.

Only someone who knew this place would have been able to find the handholds and footholds, but they were there. Carefully, but with sure feet, Finn made the climb. He tested each hold before going farther. When he had climbed five feet, he gestured to Aminda. Follow.

Mimicking his positioning, she followed. It wasn't as hard as she thought it would be. The holds were there, hidden in the rock, she just hadn't seen them. It was like climbing a wet, slick ladder. The water sprayed her face and got in her eyes, but she climbed on. Patrick clambered up the rock as close to Aminda as he could and Aminda tried not to be self conscious of the way the wet trousers clung to her legs.

Fifteen feet up, Finn disappeared behind the cascade. Aminda stifled her gasp. One moment he was there, pack slung, lantern dangling from a makeshift hook. The next moment he wasn't. She continued to climb until she reached where he had disappeared. She peered to her left. Beside her was a small ledge and the gaping black hole of a cave. Finn stood in the lantern light, smiling. He beckoned her with his finger.

There was no possible way the cave would be visible below. How Finn could have found this spot was beyond her. Maybe he really was a magician.

When Patrick had joined them in the cave, dripping and tired, they sat for a moment. Each took a small swig from a bottle Finn handed around. The liquor burned her throat, but it warmed her belly. She forced herself to swallow it without coughing. Patrick smiled at the contortions on her face, but kept silent. The space they were in was barely more than five feet tall—both Patrick and Finn had to stoop.

The wet cave walls glittered as if covered in gold. Fool's gold—gold for fools. She was a fool for being here, but here she was. Aminda wondered at the insanity of this whole adventure and wondered, once again, at her father's decision to come here. Why would he follow a map found on a pub floor? What was he thinking? There was nothing on the map about a cave, or a waterfall. Had her father even gotten this far, or had he and the other men followed the number 9 looking for something nine paces from the falls? From where she sat she could see footprints in the dirt. The footsteps of many men. Was that what her father had followed? Decades-old footprints?

When they had rested briefly and they had each taken a second gulp from Finn's bottle, they stood and followed Finn farther into the cave. It was pitch black all around them—the lantern light shone only a few paces ahead. The air was damp and smelled of must. The cave widened and grew taller just before they came to the first fork. They turned left and kept walking. Another fork sprung up in front of them within seconds. They turned left again.

Four more lefts later, Aminda got the first whiff of something foul. A smell of decay, like an unwashed butcher shop.

After the eighth fork the smell had intensified. Aminda pulled her collar up around her face. And then she saw it.

What had once been a man lay stretched out in front of them. One of his arms reached toward them like he had been straining to get to the exit and fallen flat. His face, or what used to be his face, was crawling with maggots. Flies buzzed around him, angry that their meal had been disturbed.

It was the man from her vision.

A bloated maggot wriggled from his mouth and fell to the dirt floor.

Aminda gagged.

She froze, the small retching noise echoing through the cave. Finn looked sharply at her, and gestured frantically with his hand across his mouth—no noise! His eyes searched deeper into the cave, watching. The smell was almost too much. She turned away, concentrating on taking shallow breaths through her coat. Patrick pulled her to him and sheltered her with his body, stroking her hair. The sharp musky scent of his skin cut the smell of rotting flesh. She wanted to tell him about the vision. She wanted to run away from here, away from the dark evil presence that had chased this man. But she couldn't speak. And, if her father was going to live, she had to continue on.

When her breathing had settled, she turned and nodded to Finn.

They walked on, Aminda waiting for the presence deep in the cave to make itself known.

On the ninth fork, they turned right.

The stench magnified once again. Two more bodies lay crumpled on the cave floor. More maggots. More flies. Aminda fought with her stomach and with her mind. This must be where they had to dig—so she couldn't lose it. It was Finn that had placed the curse on the treasure. He had called the presence that had killed the men in the cave. What kind of madman had she followed into this hideous place? She stood as close to Patrick as decorum would allow—closer, even. His arm wrapped protectively around her as he fought with his own stomach.

She tried not to look at the dead men, but it was hard not to. The stench of their decomposing bodies filled the air. The hum of gorging flies surrounded her. Their flesh bubbled with wriggling maggots. Filthy clothes stuck to their bodies and the bones of their fingers still held the handles of their tools.

The ground had been disturbed here and several other tools were flung around the dirt. What had happened to them? Had Finn's curse just put them to sleep like her father but with no one to bathe them and feed them? Or had they died suddenly, their hearts stopping from fear, scrambling to leave?

Her questions would have to wait.

Finn dropped his bundle on the ground and set the lantern on a ledge. He took one shovel from the pile and held it in his hand.

He walked to the very edge of the entrance to this room-like cavern, then began to pace towards the centre. One, two, three, four...he took ten steps and then stopped. He was between the two bodies.

He glanced at Patrick and Aminda and then pointed

downward with the shovel.

There. That was where they had to dig to save her father. Between two stinking, maggot-infested bodies. Finn pointed to the pile of tools and then back to the spot beneath him.

Aminda struggled with her revulsion but she had no choice. If Finn's book was here, here was where she would dig.

Patrick bent over and picked up the two remaining shovels from their pile. Handing one of them to Aminda, he stepped over a body and began to dig.

They dug in turns: one shovelling from inside the hole, one moving the dirt to the edge of the cavern, one resting. At some point in the process Patrick attempted to move one of the bodies out of the way. He grasped its arm and tried to pull. The arm detached in his hands. He carefully laid the arm down beside its owner, went to the edge of the cavern and quietly vomited the contents of his stomach onto the floor.

They dug for nearly an hour. Finally, when they were all three covered in sweat and muck, Finn struck something hard. He dug around it. He glanced warningly at Patrick, and then slowly lifted his shovel to the surface.

The shovel held another man's head.

Aminda wanted to scream. She wanted to yell and cry and faint. She slapped her hand over her mouth and bit her finger. Her eyes were wide with revulsion. Patrick looked like he might pass out. Finn merely scowled.

Grubs and crawling things squirmed in the eye sockets of the skull. Lank, dirty hair fell from it as Patrick hurled it away from him. He wiped his hands on his trousers and his face on his coat. He breathed slow and deep.

It was the last of the four who had set out with her father. Buried when the curse was triggered in a forgotten grave.

They struggled to get what remained of him out of the hole. Aminda was positive she would never be able to eat again. Bits and pieces of flesh mixed with mud and rock piled beside the hole. She left them there.

When Aminda thought she could take no more buzzing of flies and crawling of maggots, they once again struck something solid. Patrick stopped, fearful of what else he would find in the pit. Finn gestured to continue.

He lifted his shovel and dug deep. A hollow thunk echoed through the cave—the sound of wood, not bone. He bent down and dusted off a small box, then lifted it to the surface. Finally, the treasure chest! It was wooden, intricately carved and inlaid with what looked like gold. It was very heavy—too heavy for just a book.

Aminda was so relieved she could have cried.

They took the chest, leaving the bodies to rot in peace. Aminda was thankful of Patrick's solid presence beside her. One didn't generally turn one's backs on corpses. She half expected to meet their ghosts on the way out of the cave.

Each sound was magnified in the dark cavern. Their footsteps, their breathing...at times Aminda felt a dark draught crawl down her neck, like fingers, touching and searching. She turned, desperately fighting the urge to scream. No one was there.

She heard whispers. Soft moaning voices calling her name. But only Patrick and Finn walked with her in silence. Perhaps the whispers were the echoes of water rushing above. Aminda shivered, repeating the same thing over and over in her head. *They're not real. They're not real. Don't turn around. They're not real...* But still she couldn't block out the feeling of being followed.

Patrick grabbed her arm in warning as she heard it. Garbled and unearthly, the voice of the dead stood behind her.

"Back...turn back...Aminda..."

The barest of touches grazed her neck.

Aminda spun around, eyes wide in the flickering light, and opened her lips to scream. Sensing her movement, Finn lurched back and clapped his hand over her mouth. In front of her stood one of the corpses, its head lolling on its neck. A maggot rolled out of its eye socket. Patrick rubbed her shoulder. Finn tapped her arm. Every nerve in her body stood on end.

"Turn...back..." what was left of the corpse's mouth said in a dripping moan. "Come...Aminda."

Her heart was going to fly out of her chest. The corpse's bloated hand reached up—reached for her neck, touching, grabbing, pulling...

...And then dropped. Just dropped. Aminda looked down at what it had touched.

Patrick's cross.

Aminda watched in disbelief as the corpse collapsed into a stinking pile in the dirt. Finn glared at her, tugging at her arm. *I must not speak, I must not speak,* she thought over and over again. She grabbed the cross and held it tight. Patrick joined Finn, tugging her toward the exit, sweat beading his forehead. They turned, ducked their heads and ran.

Fork after fork they turned until at last they could hear the waterfall. The air freshened. Cool breezes brushed their faces. And then Finn McKeen, hampered by a chest the size of a loaf of bread, slid along the ledge and out onto the rocky wall.

Aminda slipped several times on her way down, from shaking fingers and exhaustion. It was so hard not to scream, not to cry. *There was a dead man! A dead man who talked!* Didn't they see that? How could they not be screaming? But Finn's face remained stern. They walked slowly along the beach, and she was at least glad of the fresh clean air, glad that the ordeal was almost over. But they weren't back to the mill yet.

The moon was slowly setting in the western sky as they stumbled into the boat and Patrick began the long, weary paddle back to the mill, lips sealed by fear of the curse. Aminda held Patrick's cross in her shaking hand and tried not to think. A dead man had touched her neck.

Splash, drip. Splash, drip. Splash, drip.

Finn took over rowing for a while so Patrick could rest. They all dozed in turn, but maintained their silence. Clouds were visible in the west but the moon still shone just above them, as if daring the clouds to come closer as it fell. The grey shadows of trees and rocks slipped by on the shore.

Finally, after an eternity of splashing and dripping, they rounded the corner and turned up the stream toward the mill.

CHAPTER 11

FLAME

AMINDA HAD NEVER BEEN SO happy to see the mill. It loomed in the dying moonlight as large and as ominous as ever, but it signified the end of their ordeal. Home. They were almost there. Almost safe.

Suddenly a lantern flared and a man stepped out in its light. A tall, dark man who Aminda knew in an instant. Josiah Cameron. His grin was evil and he held Caroline by the arm. Caroline's dress was ripped. Her face was bloody.

"Aminda!" Caroline's scream ripped across the water. "Help!"

Josiah's fist caught Caroline on her cheek. She doubled over and lay still, a puddle on the ground. He waved the lantern, taunting the weary travellers as they approached.

Patrick grasped Aminda's arm so she wouldn't cry out. Finn's eyes flashed.

That wretch! That lecherous bastard!

All of the hatred she had boiled into Aminda's eyes, but she didn't speak. Patrick rowed strong and fast towards the shore, his anger propelling him forward.

"You've brought me my treasure, I see," Josiah taunted.

"I'm a bartering man. Let's say we make a trade. This little strumpet's life for a chest of gold. Oh, and you Miss Ingerham, will come with me. Willingly. Worth it, don't you think?" He flashed a butcher's knife in the lantern's glow and waved it like a sword. Then he casually flicked his wrist toward Caroline.

Aminda would have growled if she could.

"What's the matter, cat got your tongue? What about you, O'Brien? You've always been a reasonable sort. Although I question your judgement now, hooking up with a witch like my Ingerham."

Patrick gave one final pull of the oars and the boat slammed into the shore. Finn jumped out and pulled the boat up. Patrick and Aminda leapt from the boat and onto solid ground as fast as they could. Their feet crunched in the pebbles on the shoreline.

Patrick grabbed Finn by the arm and pulled him around so they were face to face. He pointed at his mouth, then gave an urgent flap of his fingers. Was it safe to talk?

"Yes. It is done. Go." He said quietly. "I will help as I can."

Patrick dropped everything and ran.

Hearing Finn mutter something, Aminda turned before diving into the woods behind Patrick. Finn's lips were moving fast and in his hand, unbelievably, a fireball was forming. It swirled and shimmered like it was alive.

Fire.

Aminda had just a second to register what it meant before he sent it hurtling through the air at Josiah. Through the air toward the mill.

"No!" she screamed.

But it was too late. The ball flew through the air like musket shot. It grazed Josiah's arm and then slammed into the wall of the mill.

The dry wooden siding burst into flames.

Aminda watched in horror as Patrick came crashing through the trees and right into the stunned Josiah. The two hit the edge of the doors with enough force to knock them off their hinges. They careened through the gap and onto the mill floor, lost in the darkness beyond. Caroline lay on the ground, unmoving.

The fire on the mill wall was spreading. Small swathes of fire grew as they stole their way upward along the boards. Aminda took one last look at Finn before running into the trees toward the mill. Her vision replayed in her head over and over as she ran, ignoring the branches that whipped across her face. She had to stop it! They would both die!

And Caroline! What had Josiah done?

She ran to her cousin first. There was too little time! Her mill was burning!

Heat radiated from it like a wall of evil. What could she do?

The buckets. They were inside. She'd check Carrie and then get to the buckets. She dropped to her knees by her cousin and rolled her over carefully.

Caroline was in her nightshirt. Josiah must have stolen her from her house somehow. A rip rent the shirt from the neck toward the arm. What was left barely covered her shoulder. Aminda checked her over in the flickering light. One of Caroline's eyes was swollen. Blood trickled from a cut on her forehead. She whimpered as Aminda gently touched her bruised eye.

"Aminda?" she asked, her voice barely a whisper.

"It's okay sweetheart," Aminda replied. "I'm here. Patrick is here too. It's going to be okay. Everything will be all right."

"There's fire," Caroline said. "Smoke."

"Yes, it's the mill. Are you hurt?" Aminda scanned her cousin by the flickering light but there was no other sign of injury.

"I'm okay. He came to my house in the dark. I tripped trying to get away from him. And he ripped my nightshirt. But that's all. Until we got here."

Aminda quickly moved her farther away from the burning wall. "Is your face okay? He punched you pretty hard."

Caroline managed a weak smile. "But I got him first. My knee. His...private parts."

Aminda smiled back. "Hang in there. I've got to go. Be right back."

"Aminda, don't! Don't go in there. The fire...and Josiah! He's got a knife!"

"I'll be okay. I need to get Patrick out of there."

Caroline lay painfully back down on the ground. "Be careful."

Aminda nodded. As she rose, something whistled through the air above her. There was an explosion, and then water started dripping from the roof.

Her barrels! Finn must have seen them! The water would help.

She waved at Caroline before she darted into the burning mill.

The only light inside was the red glow of fire. Shadows and tongues of flames danced all around. Aminda ran to the first barrel she saw, filled two buckets and splashed them on the burning wall. The flames dimmed, but as they lowered others grew. She dipped and splashed until the barrel was empty, oblivious to anything but her struggle against the flames and the heat.

She moved to the next barrel, emptying it. And then the next. It wasn't helping! She needed more water and more people. Where were the villagers when she needed them?

Above her there was a large crash. Sharp cursing cut through the rustling fire.

"Patrick!" She screamed. A heavy thump shook the floor.

She filled her buckets and splashed up the stairs to the wood loft.

There was so much smoke and fire, it was hard to see. Buckets or not, Aminda knew she wasn't going to win this battle. She had to get out. But she had to find Patrick first.

"Patrick!" she screamed again into the crackling flames. "Where are you? We have to get out! Now!" She coughed and covered her face with her arm while she searched the dim, smoky room, but there was no sign of either Patrick or Josiah.

"Aminda go!" he answered over the din. "Get out!"

She was not losing him and the mill on the same night.

"No! Patrick you have to come now!"

She heard the chuckle just before the arm wrapped around her neck.

"Well, isn't this sweet," Josiah's voice rasped in her ear. She felt the sharp coldness of a blade against her neck. "Your lover boy, come to fight for you and your little brat of a cousin. She'd be a nice little treat for a man like myself, now wouldn't she?"

He was insane. "Leave Caroline out of this," Aminda replied through gritted teeth.

The hand that wasn't holding the knife slid down from her shoulder to her breast, pinching and grabbing. Pain and smoke brought tears to her eyes. Josiah laughed.

"Tsk, tsk," he said. Aminda could smell the acrid sweetness of alcohol over the smoke. He was drunk.

"Shame on you, wearing men's trousers. Only whores wear men's clothing. And we all know what whores want." Aminda didn't dare move. She could feel her skin splitting as the knife moved against her throat. That and the revolting pressure of his body behind her.

Ever so slowly, she inched her hand toward her pocket. The

handle of Patrick's hunting knife was right there. Almost...

"Maybe your lover boy can watch while I show him what a real man can do," he hissed in her ear, pushing his body rudely against her. Aminda tasted bile in the back of her throat. Her hand slipped in her pocket and grabbed the knife.

There were several more crashes overhead. Finn must have hit more of the barrels. She barely heard the trickle of water as it rolled down the shingled roof above.

Josiah's knife slipped downward as he drunkenly groped at her waist. His blade dropped, resting loosely on her chest through Finn's black coat. Aminda writhed to get away but Josiah's grip tightened. The knife in her own hand was useless with its sheath still covering it.

And then suddenly there was a thud behind her. Josiah's arms jerked and then went completely limp. His knife clattered to the floor and his arms slid away as he crumpled, nearly pushing Aminda over as he fell.

Aminda stumbled forward and whirled to see Patrick standing there. His face was covered in soot and blood trickled from his nose. He looked like a black devil in the flickering light but his face showed concern, not hatred.

"Are you okay?" he asked. His eyes went to her throat. Aminda could feel the wetness of blood there.

"I think so. It's just a scratch. Are you?"

"Nose is broken. Nothing that time won't fix." He hesitated for a moment, then lifted his hand to brush away the blood on her neck. The cut was shallow but it stung as he touched it. She winced and choked on her sudden intake of smoke.

Aminda would have loved to succumb to her want and just stand there holding him but the situation was escalating rapidly. Flames engulfed most of the northern wall. Smoke trailed along the ceiling. She coughed, squeezed his hand and shook her head.

"We've got to get out!" She ran to the barrels and dipped the buckets, throwing water at the fire as she headed for the stairs. Patrick was only seconds behind her. The crackle of flames was growing, and the roar of something else. It sounded like...rain outside on the roof. And a rush of water trickling down the walls.

She couldn't stop to think. Coughing and covering their faces the best they could, they sloshed the buckets, spraying in front of them to make a path. And then... an angry scream rose above the din.

Aminda whirled just in time to see Patrick deflect Josiah's knife.

It was the scene from her vision.

Josiah with murder in his eyes, lit by flames as he fought with Patrick. Patrick's face bloody and determined. They circled each other, testing, taunting. Josiah feinted with his knife and Patrick danced out of the way. All the while the flames rose higher and more smoke filled the air.

"Aminda, go!" Patrick yelled over his shoulder. But she shook her head. She wouldn't leave without him. She waved her knife at him, but his eyes never left Josiah.

"I know your secrets, Ingerham," Josiah hissed from the side of his mouth. "I know the evil you do. I'll beat it out of you when we get out of here. But first, O'Brien's going to pay for messing with what wasn't his."

Josiah swung again, aiming for Patrick's chest but Patrick jerked out of his way and struck out himself, landing a strong blow on Josiah's cheek.

Josiah bellowed, eyes aflame with more hate than reflection. He wiped blood from the corner of his mouth and spat. The click of a tooth hitting the wooden floor was lost in the hiss of the flames. His face contorted like one possessed.

"You filthy mick! How dare you!" The knife flashed in the

firelight as he swung again and missed.

Aminda searched for a better weapon to throw to Patrick. She still had her knife, but how could she get it to him in the flailing arms and feet? A spiked peavey hook leaned against the wall beside her and she grabbed it. She looked back just as Josiah swung his knife once more.

The night of rowing and digging had fatigued Patrick. He moved too slowly. This time the knife sunk into his arm, slicing bone-deep.

"No!" Aminda screamed, and ran towards Patrick. Josiah sneered as Patrick fell to his knees.

She knelt down beside him, laying the peavey and her knife on the floor. Josiah's hideous laughter taunting behind her.

Even in the heat of the fire, Patrick looked pale.

"What can I do?" she whispered.

He grimaced as he reached over and slipped his grandfather's hunting knife in his weak, injured hand. In the other he grasped the peavey. Blood poured from the edge of his wound.

Josiah was cursing and jeering behind her. She ignored him.

"When I yell 'now'," Patrick said quietly, "get out of the way as fast as you can. Okay?"

Aminda nodded.

She could hear Josiah's footsteps coming closer. "Aren't you going to give your lover a good-bye kiss before I finish him off?" Josiah taunted. "Or are you saving yourself for a real man?" He was right behind her. Aminda balanced on the balls of her feet, ready to spring and move.

"Now!"

Aminda threw herself to the right with everything she had. In one swift movement Patrick yanked both the knife and peavey upwards and jabbed toward Josiah.

Josiah had been reaching down to grasp Aminda by the hair. Surprise at her unexpected movement unbalanced him. He teetered and fell forward…directly onto Patrick's weapons.

Josiah groaned, eyes wide with surprise. Blood spilled from his mouth and he collapsed on top of Patrick's damaged arm.

Patrick pulled his arm out from underneath Josiah, gasping at the pain. Blood spurted from his arm wound. A flaming beam creaked and bent behind him, threatening to fall. The heat was intensifying.

Aminda rushed back to his side and frantically ripped at her shirt. She tied a makeshift bandage over his arm, now slippery with blood.

"We have to get out," she said as she worked, fingers shaking. "The ceiling's going to collapse. Can you walk?"

He nodded weakly and coughed. His face was glistening with sweat.

She helped him stand, glancing at Josiah. There was no way she could help Patrick get out and save Josiah at the same time. She would come back for him if she could. Depraved lunatic or not, she didn't want him to die.

But as they hobbled down the stairs through the flames and heat, the choice was taken away from her. The beam gave way with an ominous crack and the fiery roof came crashing down in a rain of sparks and smoke. They fled through the door and into the pre-dawn darkness, leaving Josiah Cameron to burn.

CHAPTER 12

RAIN

FINN MCKEEN WAS SITTING WITH Caroline, both of them watching the building anxiously. Aminda helped Patrick over to them and collapsed down on the ground. She sat beside them, numb from shock and fatigue, eyes captured by the sight in front of her. Facing her livelihood as it went up in flames.

She couldn't speak. The whole night was a bizarre nightmare—and now this. Years of hard work disintegrating in front of her eyes. Her poor father would be devastated when he saw his mill.

Patrick groaned and coughed beside her. She turned to him quickly—how could she have forgotten? His arm! He was lying on the ground, covered in blood and soot. The arm of his coat and shirt had been torn away. Finn was hovering over him, re-bandaging his arm and murmuring something under his breath. Patrick's eyes were open. Aminda wasn't sure if he was conscious or not.

Somewhere far in the distance, Aminda heard a cry go up. "Fire!"

"He'll be okay, Aminda," Caroline said quietly. "That man

with the white beard is a healer. He helped my eye." She pointed to her face. The bruising was still there, but the swelling had gone down.

Aminda nodded at her cousin, still too stunned to speak.

"I think he should check you too." Her cousin gave her a strange look. Aminda suspected she was quite a sight; men's clothing, soot covered face, blood and dirt from all sorts of things. She was so tired she felt drunk. If only she could sleep. But who could sleep after such a night? More yells echoed down from the village, louder this time.

Patrick turned his face toward Aminda. He smiled, a personal sort of smile. If her face wasn't already red from the heat, Aminda would have blushed.

Finn cleared his throat. "The villagers will be here soon. They see the smoke and the light of the fire," he said. "We'll need to tell them about young Josiah. What do you want them to hear? What shall our story be?"

Aminda sighed. The night was not over yet. "Josiah?" she said, trying to focus her foggy thoughts. "We will have to tell them a version of the truth. Tell them he kidnapped Caroline. Tell them he assaulted me. Tell them Patrick saved us from him. The fire started during the fight. And we only just got out with our lives."

"Josiah grabbed me while I was going to the outhouse," Caroline blurted out. "I didn't see him…he had his filthy hand over my mouth before I could scream. He pulled me here. But I fought."

Caroline's eyes were wide and damp. She dashed the tears away with her torn nightshirt.

"Did he hurt you…anywhere else?" Aminda said quietly, putting as much compassion into the question as she could.

"No. I fought him," Caroline sniffed, "and he was drunk. I almost got away while we waited here, but then you came…"

"You were very brave, Carrie. Just tell people the truth. Josiah was a horrible boy. People will understand." Well, she hoped they would anyway.

Aminda sighed and struggled to her feet, grabbing the lantern and walking as close to the mill as she could get. She threw it as hard as she could into the fire. They all heard the crash of tin against wood as it landed.

"The fire started from the lantern," Aminda said, looking pointedly at Finn. "Unless you have a better idea?"

He shook his head. "No, that sounds just about right. How about I take the chest and head up to your cabin? I still have work to do, and it's best I am not here when they arrive. Will you three be able to deal with them alone?"

Aminda nodded. "After tonight, I think I can deal with anything."

He took two steps and then turned back to the dirty trio. Reaching into his coat, he produced a small bundle.

"You might want these. Will save some explaining," he said.

As Finn McKeen walked away, the rain began to fall.

The Whitebeard left them then, walking calmly across the dam as if he were off to pick some daises. His black cloak floated like a moving shadow. The fire burned hot beside him but the flames were lowering. The wet wood of the dam wouldn't light. Finn lifted the sluice gates, and water splashed from the wheel onto the flaming mill. With the rain, and the water of the stream, and perhaps a bit of Finn's magic, the fire was dying. The top floors of the mill were destroyed but the water works were safe. The thirty-two logs floating in the headpond would have to wait.

Aminda was glad Finn McKeen had gone. She was at a loss as to how to feel about the strange man. He had helped them, yet he was the cause of the devastation in front of them. Her father's livelihood, up in smoke. And four men lay in an unmarked grave because of him.

She shuddered, partially from the memory of the talking corpse and partially from the rain dripping down her neck. She was sure the night had been clear as they approached the mill, before they had seen Josiah. Had Finn caused the rain?

And the origin of all of this chaos still began with Finn. Without him, there would be no treasure, there would be no treasure hunt and her father would never have been cursed. Yet she was confident the Whitebeard would save her father from his endless sleep. Her brain spun with cause and effect. It was too much to think about right now.

She huddled with Caroline and Patrick under a tree, as the rain accomplished what she could not. She ripped open the parcel, and was surprised to find clothing. A dress for her, and a fresh, undamaged nightgown for Caroline.

"Thank you," she whispered. She hadn't thought about her clothes. The villagers would question her trousers. Actually, they'd be mortified. She was already in enough hot water. She slipped into the bushes to change and then threw the black trousers into the fire. She could see lanterns bobbing down the hill. More yells echoed across the stream. Caroline quickly slipped her fresh nightdress over her head. Somehow, Finn had conjured a dress of perfect fit, with just the right amount of soot, for both of the girls.

As the first lantern emerged from the trees, Patrick rested quietly against the tree trunk. He stared at the burning mill, lost in his own thoughts and weak from exhaustion and loss of blood.

Mr. Stairs, the foreman, was the first person to come running down. He lived the closest and had seen the flickering smoke from his window in the early morning darkness. Barely stopping to check on the three bedraggled survivors, he rushed about, fetching water from the stream and uselessly pouring it onto the fire. Of course, there was nothing he could do for the mill. When he saw the obvious he stopped and stood beside them. They told their story, and he believed it without question. He offered to run for Caroline's father.

More villagers came running in nightshirts and hastily thrown on trousers. A bucket brigade was set up, drawing water from the headpond and passing it down to the ruins below. Aminda felt more than one accusatory eye glance her way, but she ignored them. Patrick pulled himself upright and somehow grabbed a bucket to help.

It seemed only minutes until Mr. Stairs was back, Aunt Mary scuttling like a goose and screaming the whole way. Aminda kept her distance, letting Caroline tell the story. There were plenty of tears, most of them Aunt Mary's, and several long and suspicious looks. Caroline was bundled in blankets and questioned till she couldn't talk. Even with their careful testimony, Mary still managed to make it look like it was Aminda's fault Josiah had attacked her daughter. Aminda wanted to point her own finger Mary's way, knowing of her aunt's hay mow trysts with Josiah's father, but she held her tongue. It would help no one. She watched in silence as Mary bundled off with her daughter, shooting evil looks over her shoulder at Aminda as she went.

One of the last people to arrive was the blacksmith, Josiah's father. This was not so easy. Josiah came by his temper and love of drink honestly. The man careened down the hill in a drunken stupor, ranting like a madman and brandishing an iron bar. It took Caroline's father, Mr. Stairs and two other men five minutes to convince him not to run headlong into the fire and then even more men to subdue him and remove his bar when he turned on Aminda. His face was pure hatred, and there was no subduing his mouth.

"Daughter of a whore! Witchssh! Murderessss!" He spat at

her, "It's you who should be burnin', not my son!" He writhed and cursed, but his captors held firm "Bewished him! Then threw him into the flames! Witch!"

His eyes bulged from their sockets. "Seize her! She murdered my son! Witchssh!"

Aminda searched the crowd in fear. Would they turn on her? Would they believe this raving madman over her? She faced them head on, determined not to back off. Eyes darkened in front of her, then turned away. Beyond them, Patrick walking her way, his face an anchor in the crimson light.

"Shut yer maw, Cameron," hissed Mr. Stairs. "Miss Ingerham is innocent. Your boy attacked young Caroline Morehouse in the night. O'Brien and Miss Ingerham saved her."

"Liar!" he screamed, beyond all reason. "Twas both of 'em! They bewished you all! The Catholic filth and heathen slut together!" He surged forward, straining against his captors, pitching curses like knives, head swivelling between her face and Patrick's.

Mr. Stairs mercifully saved them both from any more. He knocked Mr. Cameron on the head, and the man passed out cold.

The men dropped him to the ground and stepped away in disgust. Aminda shivered, partially from the damp, partially from fear—the man was as bad as his son. When Patrick came to stand beside her, it was all she could do not to crumple against him.

"I doubt he'll bother you for a while, Miss Ingerham," said Mr. Stairs. "And the men'll handle what's left of the mill. Reckon you should head up and get some sleep. And I reckon Mr. O'Brien should do the same. I'll send word to your folks, O'Brien, if you'd like. There's more of this storm to come, I'm thinkin'."

Aminda wasn't sure if it was the rain or the man lying on the ground he was talking about, but she was too tired to ask. She nodded. The mill would have to burn itself out. The only work for the mill men today was to help it to do so. There was no use for her here except perhaps to send down a new cask of rum for the noon-time dram. Mr. Stairs could take care of the rest on his own. Aminda hadn't slept for more than twenty-four hours, and she desperately wanted to see her father.

Patrick and Aminda walked away, his hand on her elbow to steady her. No one questioned them, and they didn't ask for permission. Too tired to even talk, they slowly struggled their way up the wet path and into the cabin.

When they walked through the door, Finn was sitting at the table chatting with Jonas Ingerham and sipping tea as if they were long-lost friends.

CHAPTER 13

GOLD

AMINDA STOOD AT THE DOOR, gawking at the scene in front of her.

Her father was chatting. He was sipping tea. He looked weak and old. But he was chatting and sipping tea. She was stunned.

He turned to see who was there... and then he smiled.

It was as if the dam had broken. Emotions exploded inside of her and she was crashing across the room, stumbling and laughing and crying and yelling and then she was there, in her father's arms.

She let hear tears flow like the pattering rain on the cabin roof.

It took a long time for her to regain herself. Her father smoothed her hair and said soothing things like she was still a child, and she let him. It was so good to be there—so good to be in his arms. Almost like being in Patrick's arms. Safe.

Patrick.

He had come in and was talking quietly with Finn. On the table was the chest, closed, and beside it a small book. The book was simple, bound in leather and tied with a piece of twine. It didn't look like much of anything, but Aminda knew it had saved her father's life.

She sat up and brushed away her tears. Patrick was watching her, a look of concern on his face.

"Father, I'd like you to meet Patrick O'Brien. Patrick, this is my father, Jonas Ingerham."

Her father assumed a stern, patriarchal look. "Mr. O'Brien."

"Pleased to meet you, sir." Patrick's voice broke as he spoke.

Aminda's father surprised her by continuing to speak. "Mr. McKeen has been telling me your story. It is a long one, and one of danger, bravery and loss. I owe you my thanks for restoring me to health and keeping my daughter safe."

"Sir, it was my pleasure, but the mill..."

Mr. Ingerham glanced at Finn. "He has told me of that too. No matter. We can rebuild." He shrugged his sagging shoulders.

"My daughter and my health are worth more than a hundred mills." He turned to Aminda. "I would ask your forgiveness. I went on a fool's errand with fools. I barely escaped with my life. I am so very sorry to have put you through this. Finn has told me that the villagers have not been kind. I will speak to them at the next meeting. They should be ashamed." His voice wavered, a mix of fatigue and anger.

"But first we must all sleep. Mr. O'Brien, will you rest with us awhile? Finn has offered to stay a few days to assist me in my recovery. There is a bed in the loft, I believe, young man. You and Finn can rest there. Aminda? Would you stay with me?"

Aminda hugged her father tightly. Of course she'd stay with him. She curled into a ball on his bed and was asleep in seconds.

She awoke to the smell of coffee and the sound of intense discussion. Her father, Patrick and Finn were at the table. The chest on the table was open. It appeared the rumours had been true—the chest was filled with gold.

She sat up quickly, eyes wide.

So Finn hadn't lied. There was a treasure! She had never seen so much gold in one place. Gold and gems and jewellery, all shining in the dim cabin light.

"Mr. McKeen and Mr. O'Brien have been telling me everything about how you...survived without me. Or mostly everything..." Mr. Ingerham smiled at his daughter as if he thought there were a few details that only she could fill in. "It sounds as if you have been very strong while I was...sick. How you kept the farm going, the mill going and helped Mr. McKeen...I'm very proud of you. And I have told him how my band of men discovered the footholds in the cliff...and followed the footsteps in the cave to the treasure."

Finn chuckled. "It seems my foolproof protection wasn't so foolproof. Alas."

Aminda was still having trouble getting it through her head that her father was alive and talking. That *she* was alive and talking.

"There is the question of the treasure, though," said her father. Mr McKeen wants nothing of the treasure." Finn nodded and smiled. "He has the ability to make more with his little book. I certainly want nothing of it. My friends paid for it with their lives. I had hoped...but no, I've said that Mr. O'Brien should take it. We need only enough to rebuild the mill, and perhaps some for your education and dowry. I also think some of the gold should go to the families of those men still in the cave. When I am well enough, I will take it to them.

Whatever is left over should go to Patrick. I owe him many thanks, for my life and for yours several times over. I think he should keep the rest."

Aminda nodded, her brain still foggy from the night—she wasn't even sure how long she had slept. "I agree, father. We have no use for treasure." It seemed as if it was all decided.

"I disagree," said Patrick simply. "I don't want it."

That was curious. Of the three entities: Mr. McKeen, the Ingerhams and the O'Brien's, the O'Brien's definitely needed it the most. They had started from nothing. They had a growing farm, but they still had very little. Why wouldn't Patrick want the gold? With that much gold, he could even move back to Ireland and set up a small estate!

"But, why not?" Aminda asked as she slid off the bed and walked to the table, still dressed in Finn's conjured clothing. "With this, you could do anything! You could go just about anywhere!" Aminda peered into the chest. It was full of more coins. It was more riches than she had ever seen, and more riches than she would probably ever see again. Somewhere in her mind was the thought of what she could do with all of that money...but she didn't need it, and really, she didn't want it. This gold had come at a huge price.

"I don't want you to give me the gold. I want you to keep it." Patrick said. "It wouldn't make me happy. My father would take it. Spend it all probably, on drink and gambling. The only thing I need to buy right now is a new plough. Although I'm sure by the time I return to the house, my parents will have already heard about my falsehood..." He grimaced, obviously more upset by the lie he'd told than by the fact that he could have been killed last night. She'd heard about Catholic guilt but had never seen it in action.

Her father chuckled.

"If it's a plough you want, you can take ours. It's in the

barn. You can take it in the cart. I'm sure Aminda would oblige me and show you where it is. But the gold is yours if you would have it. Now...I think I may attempt a stroll down to the mill. Finn, if you'd assist me, I'd be in your debt."

"Certainly. It would be my pleasure," Finn replied.

Their chairs scraped back and her father stood. His clothes hung on his frame, but his back was straight. Aminda noticed a new streak of grey in his hair. He stepped slowly towards the door, his arm resting on Finn's shoulder. He had aged ten years in the past two weeks.

Patrick sat silently across from her as they watched her father walk out the open door and down the stairs.

"Your father is a good man," Patrick said quietly. "He loves you very much."

"I know," she said.

It was hard to watch her father so. He had always been so strong—through the loss of her mother, the struggle of their journey and the tedious work of rebuilding their lives.

A gentle touch roused her from her reverie. Patrick's work-roughened fingers brushed her knuckle.

Aminda blushed. His touch aroused things in her that she hadn't known existed until recently.

They were alone.

"I believe you were to show me a plough?" he asked, grinning.

"Oh, yes. A plough."

She stood up with a jerk, trying to maintain some sort of control over her emotions. The familiar something was awakening in her stomach. It was once again very warm in the cabin. Patrick and heat seemed to go hand in hand.

"It's in the barn." Did he know what he did to her? Did the same thing happen to him?

"Shall we go and look for it?" he asked.

It was a good thing one of them was thinking straight.

She stepped into her barn clogs and out into the late afternoon sun. From the veranda she could see her father and Finn on the small bridge that crossed the dam. Her father held both handrails. Finn trailed closely behind.

Patrick followed her to the barn. Shadow whickered a hello. Aminda felt a pang of guilt—she hadn't done any chores today.

"Sorry, Shad. It's been a bit crazy today," she said. She led the horse to the paddock. She still had to milk their cow, Daisy, who lowed anxiously from her stall.

Patrick chuckled.

"I'll help. I think the plough can wait."

They set to work. The milking and feeding and cleaning went by quickly with the two of them, both lost in their thoughts, both thinking similar things.

When the last stall had been cleaned out and the barn set to rights, Aminda leaned on her fork and smiled at Patrick.

He reached forward and brushed a smudge from her cheek.

"I spoke long and hard with your father while you were sleeping, Aminda. I...told him of my feelings for you. He listened. Finn vouched for me."

The light caught his eye lashes. He looked up at the ceiling boards, then down again.

"I know we come from different places—different worlds. But the last week has been more than I could imagine. You are so beautiful..." He stroked her cheek. "...And strong, and smart, and damn it I don't care if you're Catholic or not. When Josiah had you in that burning mill I knew I would rather die than have his hands on you."

Aminda was silent but her heart was beating louder than the millworks.

"So, I...I told your da that. I told him, and we talked and..."

Patrick knelt down and pulled a large, sparkling diamond ring from his pocket while Aminda watched in shock.

"Aminda Jane Ingerham...will you marry me?"

EPILOGUE

I T WAS A FINE DAY as Finn McKeen set out from the Port of Halifax. The breeze was stiff, and the sails filled as the ship left the bay. He was hopeful. Hopeful that he would find his dear Colleen. Hopeful that his life-long love was still living, still waiting. And if she wasn't? What would he do?

His beard whipped around his face, and the deck swayed in the rolling waves. He took out his book and looked at it, deep in thought. He had left the young lovebirds weeks ago, but somehow they were caught in his head. It had surprised him how quickly he had grown to like them. A pretty little thing, Miss Aminda, and her gift of the Sight was strong. With some training...no, it was not to be. He had no time for an apprentice now.

He looked to the sky, and his weather sense told him the sun would continue to shine long into the week. A seagull cried above the ship, swirling in the over-bright ocean sky.

The foreboding hit him strong and clear.

Danger. Not for him but for the young beauty. The seagull's cry echoed in his head as the girl screamed. His hand flew to his temple. He saw Aminda lying on the ground, eyes closed.

He turned, panic stricken, as the shoreline faded in the distance.

It was too late. He couldn't turn back now. Aminda

Ingerham was on her own.

THE END

AUTHOR'S NOTES

I N THE EARLY 18TH CENTURY, many loyalists to the British Empire emigrated from the northern United States to eastern Canada. They settled along the ocean, bays and waterways, gradually working their way up the Saint John River to Sainte Anne's Point and Kingsclear, where this story is set. Ste Anne's Point was renamed Fredericton when it became the provincial capital of New Brunswick in 1785.

Today, on a stretch of the river near Kingsclear, there lies a wonderful place called King's Landing Historical Settlement; a living museum where costumed interpreters spend their days cooking on open hearth fires and woodstoves, hammering square nails at the forge and working in a sawmill set on a creek just up from the river. All of the homes there were moved to save them from destruction when the Mactaquac power dam was built and the upper Saint John River Valley was flooded. My father works there, and has been an invaluable resource as I formed my story around the setting.

Though the characters are fictional as is the placement of the homes in this story, many of the family names used in *Treasure in the Flame* were surnames of the original settlers in the area, and some of the names of the homes you will find at King's Landing. The names Morehouse, Joslin, Stairs and Cameron can all be found on early 19th Century census registers.

One of the homes at King's Landing, the Killeen Cabin, is set way off from the main road. The Killeen family (from which Patrick O'Brien in my story emerged) was granted a less accessible piece of land because they were Irish and Catholic. They were required to build their own road, and were poorer and lived rougher than the rest of the village.

There are many legends of pirate gold and buried treasure in the Canadian Maritimes. The most famous is the Oak Island treasure. *Treasure in the Flame* is based loosely on a such a legend told to me by my father. On the Koac (said KOH-ack) Stream near Nackawic (said NACK-ah-wick), it is said that a man buried one of his pirate stashes. The treasure was cursed. A small group of men, certain of the treasure's location, set out one night to retrieve it. The rumour was that those who dug for the treasure had to go in the dark of night and dig in complete silence. The men dug silently through the night...until one of their shovels thunked on a hollow box. In his excitement, one of the men cried out, "There it is!" And the pit collapsed upon them, killing them all.

Of course, if they all died...who told the story in the first place?

Aminda's idea of rain barrels on the roof really was used, although, as in this story, it's unlikely they were much help in a real fire.

And foremen (like Aminda in this story) really did hand out a dram of rum at lunch time and at quitting time. A dram is the equivalent of about a fifth of a cup, but in early North American sawmills it was probably more. Not a bad way to end a hard day's work!

ACKNOWLEDGEMENTS

THIS STORY, LIKE ALL STORIES, started as an idea. That idea blossomed after a visit to Kings Landing Historical Settlement, and became a manuscript in November of 2010, thanks to the guilt-ridding wonders of NaNoWriMo—a world-wide novel writing program in which writers pledge to complete a 50,000 word novel in a mere thirty days. One does not write a manuscript in thirty days without help and encouragement. Nor does one turn a manuscript into a published novel without truckloads full of the same. So...

To the NaNoWriMo folks who read my drivel and said good things about it, thank you. Your encouragement kept the momentum going. To my online critique group friends who I still meet with online from time to time—your kind words kept me on the right track. To my editor, the amazing Jesse Steele and the folks at The Editorial Department, thank you for finding those commas and helping them disappear. To my proof-reader, Wendy Dunlop Marr, thank you for finding even more commas, and helping *them* to disappear. And to the folks at Streetlight Graphics, thank you for your understanding as I floundered through the process of cover design and formatting.

Thank you to my wonderful Mom, who read my draft and praised my efforts, and also to my talented Father, who knows about sawmills, streams and legends, took pictures and answered countless questions about the workings of a late 18th/early 19th Century village.

To my dear friend Vicki, who has supported me more than she knows, you're the best.

To my three stupenderific children—you are why I write. Watching you explore the wonderful world of the printed page fills me up with happiness.

And lastly, to my husband, who came back from five stressful months in the desert to a wife surgically connected to her laptop—thank you for lifting me up when I fall, for helping me move forward when I need a push, and for loving me through it all.

14425193R00100

Made in the USA
Charleston, SC
10 September 2012